W9-CIG-508

JERICHO
MAN

Books by John Lutz

JERICHO MAN

LAZARUS MAN

BONEGRINDER

BUYER BEWARE

THE TRUTH OF THE MATTER

JERICHO MAN

by
John Lutz

WILLIAM MORROW AND COMPANY, INC.
New York   1980

Copyright © 1980 by John Lutz

All rights reserved. No part of this book may be reproduced or utilized in any form or by any means, electronic or mechanical, including photocopying, recording or by any information storage and retrieval system, without permission in writing from the Publisher. Inquiries should be addressed to William Morrow and Company, Inc., 105 Madison Ave., New York, N. Y. 10016.

Library of Congress Cataloging in Publication Data

Lutz, John, 1939-
  Jericho man.

  I. Title.
PZ4.L977Je   [PS3562.U854]   813'.54   80-14988
ISBN 0-688-03719-4

Printed in the United States of America

First Edition

1 2 3 4 5 6 7 8 9 10

For Ralph and Eunice Pope

PROLOGUE

1974

The bare steel framework of the Morgell Trust Building loomed like a boxy, symmetrical skeleton hundreds of feet into the cloud-shredded night sky. Recent rains had stymied work on the building, but still construction was ahead of schedule. Earlier that day the steel skeleton had been swarmed over by dozens of hard-hatted workers, and the cranes that now sat by idly had racketed with engine and hydraulic-lift noises as they cable-hoisted tons of material to the riveters above.

But now the construction site was silent, deserted. The building was going up on East Fifty-fourth Street, in an area of Manhattan that was almost exclusively commercial. At this time of night the streets were dark, empty and dangerous. Frequently one of the ever-present yellow cabs swished past on the wet pavement, but there were few pedestrians. In the towering buildings, surrounding the site of the future Morgell Trust Building, a galaxy-like scattering of lights still shone in high windows. At a corner a block away the neon sign of an all-night lounge cast a shimmering red gloss over the wet street, but there were no cars parked outside the lounge and its business seemed nonexistent.

On East Fifty-fifth, adjacent to the Morgell construction site, a battered blue '65 Ford pulled to the curb. The engine stopped, leaving the windshield wiper arms extended over the rain-beaded glass like motionless insect antennae. For a long time the driver sat behind the steering wheel, then he scooted to the passenger's side.

He began to open the door but sat still when a cab glided past, its white dome light glowing. When the cab had turned the corner, the man got out of the Ford, opened a rear door and removed two large leather suitcases. He closed the car door without slamming it, looked up and down the empty street, then picked up the suitcases in a manner indicating that they were quite heavy and disappeared into a narrow alleyway that led toward Fifty-fourth Street and the rear of the Morgell Trust Building construction site.

The site was crudely fenced in with unpainted warped plywood, and the man with the suitcases had little trouble finding a seam and prying loose one of the damp, splintery panels. He pushed the suitcases in ahead of him, then, with a quick glance around, squeezed through the opening himself and pulled the plywood panel back into place.

Heavy rain had stopped falling almost an hour ago, but an intermittent mist had set in, and the darkly dressed figure with the suitcases shivered noticeably as it made its way over muddy ground to planks laid end to end to form a walkway across the muck. The dark figure strode with easy balance over the planks toward the vast concreted foundation cavity that would form the building's basement garage.

From the incompleted steel and stonework above came a faint metallic clinking sound—something falling from up high. The man with the suitcases froze for a moment, gazing skyward, but he knew there could be no one above. He continued across the mud-caked planks and merged with the darkness of the foundation cavity.

8

The cement floor of the foundation had been poured. It was littered with debris—irregularly sawed pieces of lumber, snakelike lengths of frayed cable, stacks of wooden cement forms. About everything was a damp, rancid odor. Deep puddles of muddy water lay in wide patterns between thick vertical supporting beams, some of which had already been wrapped with insulation to protect conduit and ductwork.

After resting the suitcases on the cement floor, the man shone a flashlight beam quickly about. He located the electrical terminals, then the huge boilers that had been lowered into position by crane the week before. The flashlight beam played over parallel lines of pipe, concrete walls still bristling with steel snap ties, then abruptly winked out.

The man stood still for a moment, letting his eyes adjust to the unbroken darkness. He placed masking tape over the lens of the flashlight to narrow the beam, so that he could shield the light with his body for close work. Then he got busy.

An hour later, the darkly dressed man emerged from the alley onto Fifty-fifth Street, near where the battered Ford was parked. He turned up the collar of his blue windbreaker, then carried the suitcases—effortlessly now—to the car, opened a rear door and tossed them onto the floor behind the front seat.

He was walking around to get into the car on the driver's side when the wino approached.

The wino was tall but stooped, wearing a plastic raincoat that looked as if it had been tattered by the wind like a distressed kite. The coat was too short, making his wrinkled pants legs and mud-spattered shoes seem incredibly oversized. Above the coat, which was buttoned to his chin, was a grizzled lantern jaw and hopeless rheumy eyes.

"A minute of your time, brother," the wino said, blocking the way in calculated subservience. "I could sure use whatever change you might spare. It'd give me enough for a place to sleep."

"Sorry," the darkly dressed man said, moving to walk around to the street.

"Then enough for something hot to drink. Hey, it's a miserable night, you noticed?" Long fingers raked through scraggly wet hair.

"You got the wrong customer," the man said, pushing the wino gently aside.

The wino clutched at the man's arm and started to beg in earnest, but a fist darted out and with a muted snapping sound jolted the grizzled chin to one side. The wino staggered back several steps with splayed fingers pressed to the side of his jaw. He looked scared and righteously indignant.

The man in the old Ford drove away faster than was necessary. His heart was beating wildly and unevenly as he slowed to cross an intersection, then drove west toward Sixth Avenue. It didn't matter about the drunk, he knew, but the incident had frightened him because he hadn't planned on anything like that happening. No matter how carefully you planned, or how far into the future, something unexpected could always happen. When the stakes were high, the unexpected was a constant concern.

He was still jittery as he waited for the traffic light at Sixth Avenue.

To calm himself, he turned on the car radio and punched one of the plastic pushbuttons. The rain began falling heavily again. He heard the somber voice of Richard Nixon: "I will under no circumstances resign . . ."

Here was the President of the United States, the man thought, and *he* hadn't been able to plan carefully enough.

He punched another button and got the sort of soft music he didn't really like. But tonight it soothed him.

The light blinked green and he accelerated.

It was the complex or hastily conceived plans that failed. And his was neither of those.

It would be all right, he told himself, lighting one of the strong cigars that the doctor had told him to give up. Everything would be all right. If not in a short while, eventually.

10

1

The Morgell Trust Building, completed for seven years, dominated its side of the block on East Fifty-fourth. Its blanched stone face swept back gracefully from the front building line to maintain a satisfying distance from the street in relation to its height, then soared almost straight up for forty stories. In the clear, bright morning, the building appeared still new and clean, and on its eastern tiers of cast concrete and smooth, copper-burnished panels, hundreds of orange, distorted morning suns glared back at the genuine sun just rising to clear the shadowed, jagged skyline.

On the ground floor were the main branch of Morgell Trust, Melori's Restaurant (now serving breakfast), a men's apparel shop, a bookstore and the offices of Carlton and Favor Brokerage. These establishments were located on the perimeter of an ornately tiled and paneled lobby on one side of which were rows of stainless steel elevator doors. The upper floors, not entirely leased, were sectioned off into office space. The plush and gleaming offices of Morgell Trust occupied the entire top floor.

On the sidewalk outside the building, Felipe (Iggy) Gomez gracefully balanced a covered tray of danish above his head with one extended, seemingly triple-jointed arm as he wended his way along the crowded pavement, then, remarkably, through the revolving doors into the Morgell Trust Building's lobby. It was seven fifty-five; he was late. While aware of this, Iggy wasn't unduly excited.

He walked past several people waiting for the elevators, smiled at a short blonde with great-looking unfettered knockers and turned left through the entrance of Melori's.

The restaurant wasn't particularly crowded this morning; they wouldn't jump on him too heavily for being twenty minutes late with the rolls. He swerved to walk along a line of white-covered tables positioned symmetrically on the deep maroon carpet, still balancing the tray effortlessly above his head, and made his way into the kitchen. What was twenty minutes?

"Twenty minutes late," Leo the cook observed, glancing at his watch as he turned an omelet.

Iggy shrugged his bony seventeen-year-old shoulders. "I noticed everybody outside all lined up for danish."

"I noticed your smart mouth."

"You're more alert than you look."

Carello the manager walked into the kitchen. He had on his usual tight blue suit and his curly, graying hair was flopped down over his forehead to demonstrate how harried he was. Iggy saw that Carello was frowning and figured a person had to get up around fifty years old to be able to frown like that, with all the deep horizontal lines on the forehead.

"Jesus!" Carello said.

"Naw, it's me with the danish."

Carello smoothed his hair back out of his eyes. "You came through the restaurant again. I told you, didn't I, to use the rear entrance? We don't want you waltzing around among the customers with a tray of danish."

Iggy absently scratched his right testicle. "I recall some mention of it."

"You recall it all, starting tomorrow, or I'll have your fuckin' job!"

"You wouldn't want my job, Mr. Carello. The feet get tired lugging around all that food every day."

"Want me to throw hot grease on him?" Leo asked.

Carello grunted. "Why should you get such pleasure?"

"Sign here," Iggy commanded, extending an impossibly dirty receipt pad.

"You drop this?" Carello asked, scrawling his signature on the pad, then wiping his hand with a handkerchief.

"Dropped it and stepped on it. See you." Iggy handed Carello his receipt copy, lifted his right hand in a wave, tucked the pad in his pocket and walked from the kitchen. He cut again through the restaurant, where half a dozen customers were silently having breakfast, a few of them drinking coffee and reading newspapers.

Something, some perception on the very edges of the senses, caused a redheaded man sitting near the door to look up uneasily from his paper.

A moment passed.

Iggy stopped and stared, amazed.

The redheaded man was suddenly up in the air, above the table, still in a sitting position with the newspaper held in both hands in front of him. At almost the same instant, Iggy felt a great blast of air wham against him and he went flying out the double doors of the restaurant into the lobby. Also in that instant he got just an impression of at least a dozen white-faced, wide-eyed people tumbling madly toward him with arms and legs flailing, as if everything were suddenly on a steep tilt.

The atmosphere pulsed with the opening notes of unnaturally loud thunder, and as Iggy whimpered and struggled to his hands and knees, a terrifying, crushing darkness descended on him.

The Morgell Trust Building plummeted straight down upon itself, within itself.

13

The almost simultaneous explosions about the foundation had shattered windows in a half-mile radius, then sent a dark plume of debris-laden smoke crawling up one side of the building.

A long, shock-protracted second had passed.

Then another. The Morgell Trust Building had seemed to waver along its entire height, like an improbable optical illusion.

And with a growing, grating rumble, the building began to come straight down. The sound of the original explosion was as nothing compared to the steadily increasing thunderous roar as stone and steel and flesh descended mass upon mass for forty stories to a blossoming tumult of rubble and death. If there were shouts for help, they might as well have been silent shouts; if there were screams, they were lost in a maelstrom of noise. For a slowed segment of time the world consisted only of that terrifying, paralyzing roar. For miles around, the pavement quavered as it might during an earthquake.

The roar of the Morgell Trust Building's descent was heard throughout Manhattan's East Side. Those farthest away thought it was an extended, ominous peal of freakish thunder out of the clear sky. But in the skyline on East Fifty-fourth Street was a wide, unbelievable gap, jolting in its simple and sudden reality. And throughout the East Side for most of that morning hung a grayish, gritty haze held by the calm day like a grim reminder.

Within the first few hours after the explosions and the building's collapse, 423 dead and over 1000 wounded were removed from the five-story-high mass of wreckage. Countless more were buried deep within the rubble, but it would take days, and in some cases weeks, to find them. Smoldering fires kept the Fire Department busy and threatened to suffocate many of the trapped.

As the news spread, the city, the entire country, stood aghast and saddened. President Carter authorized immediate federal aid; the National Guard was activated to help reach buried survivors as quickly as possible. All that day and night, sirens singsonged and wailed like lost mourners.

In Puerto Rico, where he was vacationing at El San Juan Towers Hotel, Mayor William Danner left immediately to return to the city.

On the morning of the disaster, police captain Dexter P. Canby, who less than twelve hours ago had returned from his vacation fishing in Michigan, and who less than ten minutes ago had entered his 17th Precinct office for the first time in two weeks and was unaware of the scope of the Morgell Trust explosion, wondered if anything important had occurred during his absence.

2

Canby sat at his time-scarred mahogany desk and surveyed the stack of reports in his in basket, as well as the dusty barrenness of his gray metal out basket. He glanced around his office, feeling the steady cool draft from the laboring air conditioner mounted in the window behind him. The curtains that swayed gently in the cool rush of air cast wavering dim shadows and deceptive prisms of sunlight about the room.

The office was large and utilitarian: a bank of dented gray filing cabinets along one wall, a few uncomfortable wood chairs, a small black vinyl sofa, a cluttered work table over which was mounted a cork bulletin board papered with yellowing memos and directives. To one side of Canby's desk the standard portraits of the mayor and the governor hung mutually crooked on the wall. The walls were light green and needed paint badly.

Canby sighed. He was a tall man with a burgeoning paunch that belied an otherwise lean capability. His dark hair was still thick, though graying in uneven patches at the temples. His features were stern and he was gray-eyed and handsome

16

despite an oversized, slightly crooked nose. Possibly his most noteworthy characteristic was his hands. They were large, unnaturally still when at rest, and powerful-looking. In his hands and his finely lined features was an oddly urbane sort of ruggedness. Sighing did not become him.

Though he'd been on vacation for the past two weeks, he felt as if he'd walked out of his office only two minutes ago, then returned. From outside the office came the occasional clomp of rhythmic footsteps toward the outer door, and the monotonous metallic drone of the dispatcher's voice as it directed cars like pieces in a harrowing game played on the city's miles of streets. That anonymous voice chanted a constant background litany that was an integral part of Canby's life.

He was almost fifty now. He had started on the force twenty-eight years ago as a beat patrolman in the tough and corrupt eighteenth precinct. Canby had survived that jungle, acquired within it a steeliness and wily though direct outlook that had served him well and gained him the respect of his fellow officers. Twenty-eight years ago in the eighteenth, you either had your hand out or you were perfectly straight; there was no middle ground. Canby had played straight and been one of the few who did while managing to remain at the eighteenth and survive. He had spent eight years there and achieved a certain effectiveness and credibility with the eighteenth's inhabitants that was the secret envy of much of the force.

It was in the eighteenth that Canby gained the friendship and aid of then Lieutenant Elias Thorpe, a veteran officer ten years older than Canby and in charge of the eighteenth's burglary detail. They kept Thorpe on burglary because he was too honest for the vice squad. And they kept him in the eighteenth because he was too smart and tough to be run off. Now he was the police commissioner. It was Thorpe who had backed Canby and been responsible for his promotions through the ranks to his present position as captain. But anyone who thought those promotions were automatic didn't know Thorpe. Or Canby.

17

Canby punched the intercom button and asked the desk man to send in Lieutenant Willard Mathews. Mathews had been acting captain in Canby's absence. He was a hard-working, studious sort of cop who under pressure displayed a surprising presence of mind. Mathews had a future in the department if he avoided the pitfalls, but he might be too much of an idealist for that.

Mathews entered Canby's office with a file folder in his hand. He was a tall, rangy, thirtyish man with an awkwardness that would never leave him. His face was long, dark, bespectacled, framed by wispy brown hair that wouldn't stay combed. From the left corner of his nose and around the curve of his cheek ran a thick scar from nine years ago when as a rookie he'd tried to break up a domestic quarrel and the wife had turned on him with a paring knife. Mathews should have learned more from that than he had.

He shook hands with Canby, then sat down when Canby sat back down. Instead of asking Canby if he'd caught any fish—a question Canby already was tired of—he placed the thick yellow file folder on the desk.

"The stats for when you were gone," he said.

Canby leaned back in his swivel chair, listening for and hearing the familiar squeak. He liked Mathews' easygoing but business-first attitude. "Anything in particular I should know about?"

"A man named Shockley was booked for assault and admitted the Graham Insurance break-in. We recovered most of the money at his apartment."

"What made him confess?"

"A crying need for smack. What part of the loot he'd spent had gone to support his habit. We confiscated some of the stuff in his apartment along with the money." Mathews got out a pack of Viceroys, withdrew a cigarette deliberately and lit it. He knew Canby didn't smoke so he didn't offer. "And Frank Kelly got hurt—a broken leg and some internal injuries. Hit by a car on East Sixtieth while he was directing

18

traffic. He's in Regent Hospital but due to be released in a few days."

"I'll get up there and see him. What about this explosion on Fifty-fourth that came in a few minutes ago?"

"Not much info on it yet. McGuire is on his way there, or should be there by now. And three cars have been dispatched. You don't suppose—"

"What?"

"—that this reported explosion is what made that loud noise and caused the building to vibrate?"

"The noise, maybe," Canby said. "But Fifty-fourth is quite a way from here." He remembered the rumbling and his momentary unsteadiness as he'd entered the precinct house. He'd thought the noise might be thunder, the unsteadiness a loss of balance, or that what he'd experienced was the noise and vibration of a heavy truck going past on Fifty-first.

There was a soft knock, then without Canby's invitation the door opened and Norris the desk sergeant poked his head in. His normally florid face was unusually ruddy, and his white hair was mussed as if he'd just run his fingers through it.

" 'Scuse me, Captain, but I need help on these phones. Six kinds of hell have busted loose."

"About what?"

"That Fifty-fourth Street explosion. I'm getting wild stories. Some of these people are incoherent."

"Give him a hand until we can hail somebody," Canby ordered Mathews.

They got up and went outside into the pale green-tiled booking area, with its wide wood counter, brass grillwork and wood tables and chairs that smelled faintly of sweat and human desperation. The switchboard glittered like a symmetrical Christmas decoration.

A couple of beat patrolmen walked in just then to file a report. Canby told Mathews never mind and instructed the patrolmen to man the phones with Norris. One of the patrolmen asked Canby if he had caught any fish.

19

Within a few seconds, on what should have been a quiet morning, the aging precinct house was alive with intermingled voices. As he watched the youngest of the patrolmen take his first few calls, Canby saw the youthful face tense as if its flesh had lost all elasticity.

Norris cupped a gnarled hand over the mouthpiece of his receiver and raised his voice. "Captain! It's McGuire!"

Canby pointed to his office, motioned for Mathews. They went in and closed the door and Canby took McGuire's call on his desk phone.

"Welcome back, Captain." There was an uncharacteristic heavy irony in McGuire's voice. He was a fifty-five-year-old sergeant without a sense of humor to go with his seasoned judgment and imperturbability.

"Where are you?" Canby asked.

"On East Fifty-fourth at the Morgell Trust Building. Only there is no more Morgell Trust Building."

Canby felt a cold uneasiness as he caught the quaver in McGuire's usually steady voice. "How much damage?" Canby asked, hoping to reduce the report to dimensions more easily coped with. But he knew better.

"Total destruction, sir. Hard to believe, but the building is completely gone. I haven't seen so many dead since Korea. You'd better send everything we can spare and some we can't. Imagine it as bad as you can, sir, then imagine it worse."

"McGuire, where are you phoning from?"

"A mobile phone in a WTVU news car, on Fifty-fifth."

"What are you doing on Fifty-fifth?"

"There is no more Fifty-fourth where the building was. The street's buried under rubble so high it's banked against the buildings on both sides." The timbre of McGuire's voice changed drastically. "Jesus, Captain! . . ."

"Stay where you are. I'll meet you there."

For half a minute there was only the ocean sound of the phone connection.

"Yes, sir." McGuire's voice was normal again. "I just can't quite believe this."

Canby hung up. "He says the building's gone," he told Mathews.

"Gone? . . . What kind of building?"

"The Morgell Trust Building."

Mathews blanched. "That isn't possible . . ."

Canby's phone buzzed and his extension button blinked. He picked up the receiver.

"Dex, how was your vacation?" It was Molly Garrity, a department clerk who worked upstairs.

"I can't talk now, Molly. Something big brewing."

"I missed you, Dex." She sounded slightly puzzled by his brusqueness. "What's so important?"

"Right now I wouldn't want to try to explain. I'm not sure myself."

"All right. We can talk later."

"As soon as possible, Molly. You know that."

She said that she knew, and that she still missed him.

Canby replaced the receiver, knowing that he should have handled her call differently.

"Have Norris send everything in service to the Morgell Trust Building," he said to Mathews. "Then notify Central that the building is reported destroyed, with dead and wounded. I'm leaving to meet McGuire there."

Five patrolmen were manning the phones now and unable to do the job as Canby walked swiftly through the booking and complaint area, past the door that led to the holdover cells, then down the hall and outside.

As he stood on the concrete steps, he could hear the faraway discordant chorus of sirens; some he identified as belonging to firefighting equipment and ambulances. A talcky grayish haze had moved in, gritty enough to set his teeth on edge. It seemed to be thicker toward East Fifty-fourth Street.

"Good Christ," Canby said absently, but loud enough to startle himself.

He hurried toward where his unmarked car was parked.

3

Near the site of the explosion, the thick haze was so dark that the morning took on the dimness and consistency of dusk. Canby parked his car and walked. From a block away, through gaps between the buildings, he could see the incredible mound of rubble that at points was five stories high. Some of the people on the streets wore numbed, blank expressions that reminded Canby of photographs he'd seen of the homeless wandering about the desolation caused by military bombings. Closer to the scene of the explosion, the people were massed enough to be called a crowd, though they were eerily silent.

The nearer Canby got the more unbelievable became the destruction. He flashed his identification at a patrolman standing near where the street was cordoned off and was let past. The patrolman seemed admirably nonchalant. Or did his face display the same shocked numbness that marked many of the onlookers?

The WTVU news car was easy to find. McGuire was standing at the rear of the powder-blue car with his uniform shoe braced shiny and black on the dusty chrome bumper. He was talking to a man Canby recognized as a plainclothesman on the Mobile Reserve Squad. As Canby approached, McGuire lowered his foot and the plainclothesman diplomatically drifted away.

McGuire was a big man, rotund and powerful, with a stony face and chilling blue eyes. The saving grace of that stern face was a startlingly bright smile, but there were no smiles in McGuire this morning. He stood in an attitude of attentiveness, his thumbs hooked inside his thick black holster belt, his uniform cap tilted toward the back of his head.

"Lay it out," Canby said.

"I got six men on crowd control," McGuire replied, "but in a short while that's not going to be enough. Burnette from the fourth is here, and a couple of guys from Central. They and a few others are helping dig out survivors. They were here before the Fire Department and doing that, so I let them continue and figured I'd pull them if I needed them." As if to justify that decision, he added, "It's worse than you might think, Captain."

"More help's on the way. Let's get closer."

McGuire followed Canby as they flanked some buildings and made their way along the eastern edge of the mass of rubble, toward East Fifty-fourth. They turned a corner and Canby hesitated, awed by the extent of the wreckage and the great blank space of sky where the building had stood.

Firefighting equipment was scattered everywhere, and the debris-cluttered street near the rubble's edge was crisscrossed with pulsing snakelike hoses. There was a great deal of shouting, somehow muted by the thick haze that was being darkened by smoke from smoldering fires glowing here and there within the rubble like sinkholes into a hellish interior. Firemen in long slickers were positioned on the debris as on the slope of a mountain, playing water carefully over the fires. Carefully because they didn't want the trapped they were trying to save from death by burning or smoke inhalation to drown in rushes of water from the powerful fire hoses. Row upon row of dead, some of them uncovered, some with torn shirts or undershirts pulled up over their faces, lay on the north side of the street, and as Canby watched, rescue workers added another member to that grisly assembly. An ambulance rushed away silently, as if in respect, then cut in its siren loudly half a block away and sped with its precious cargo to the nearest hospital. Hundreds of people wandered aimlessly or sat or lay in the street, their faces and clothing marked with blood.

A third of the way up the mass of rubble, Canby saw what appeared to be a man's leg extended from beneath a blackened steel beam. Against the vastness of the wreckage, the efforts of the rescuers seemed sad and futile. Canby watched several dazed members of the crowd climb onto the rubble and begin to dig and toss aside chunks of cement and brick.

"Have them stop," Canby instructed McGuire. "They'll only get in the way of the people who know what they're doing. I'll meet you back here in five minutes." He turned and strode back the way they'd come, toward the WTVU news car.

There was a van parked near the car now. Canby used the car's mobile phone to call Mathews at the seventeenth.

"Alert everyone off duty and get them over here," Canby said.

"It's done," Mathews told him. "Orders came down from Central. And the governor's supposed to activate the National Guard to aid in rescue operations."

"We'll need all the help we can get. This is a hell of a thing." Even as he spoke, Canby was aware of the inadequacy of his words. Mathews would have to see for himself.

As if privy to Canby's thought, Mathews said, "I can leave Horn here to coordinate so I can get over there myself."

"Good idea," Canby said. "The crowd's going to be a problem soon, and these emergency vehicles have to get in and out fast."

"Are there many injured?"

"It looks as if a lot of the injured hit by debris falling onto

24

the street have been taken away, though there are plenty of them still walking around. God knows how many dead and injured are buried in what used to be the building."

"Probably mostly dead there," Mathews said dispassionately. Canby knew he was right.

"You or Horn buzz me on the pager if you need me," Canby said, and hung up.

Neal of the WTVU news room was waiting for Canby as the captain got out of the car.

"Captain Canby, do you have any idea what caused this?"

Canby paused. He knew he owed some cooperation for the use of the equipment. Apparently it would be in the form of a TV interview.

"No idea at all at the moment," he said, standing near Neal's mike and watching the shoulder-supported minicamera moved into position.

"Do you think the explosion could have been a deliberate act?"

"It's too early to think anything." Canby saw that the handsome Neal had a dark smudge beneath his left eye and on the side of his nose. Genuine? Or macabre show-biz journalism?

"I know you're busy, Captain, but could you give us some estimate as to the number of dead and injured?"

"I would if I could. Right now that's impossible. I don't see how very many inside the building could have survived." Canby began edging away, gradually turning his back on the camera.

Neal decided not to press. "Thank you, Captain." The portable TV light-bar winked out, as if signifying that it was time for a commercial.

Canby remained at the scene of the explosion until six the next morning, then, in a stupor of fatigue and blanked memories, he made his way home through the pallid, irresolute dawn.

His apartment was small, comfortable and clean, furnished with a bachelor's precision and convenience yet with a disorder here and there that stemmed not so much from sloppiness as from things going unattended. It was obvious that a man lived there who once had known a woman's care. Canby's wife Bernice had been dead almost five years now.

He walked on rubbery legs into the bedroom and tilted the blinds to block out the brightening morning light. Then he sat on the edge of the bed and removed his shoes. He knew he should phone Molly Garrity, but he was too tired, too tired even to rise from the bed. Molly would have to understand.

From outside came the distant inane song of several sirens wailing in unison. Dead and injured still were being removed from the remains of the Morgell Trust Building. It would take days to find them all. Canby swiveled his body on the mattress and lay on his back, his arms at his sides.

Strangely, the faraway, urgent notes of the sirens soothed him like an inharmonious lullaby. He fell asleep.

4

When Canby returned to his office at two that afternoon, Commissioner Thorpe was there waiting for him.

Thorpe was a heavy-set man with a thick neck and bulbous blue eyes that made him appear perpetually on the verge of anger. He had on an expensive gray suit with a conservative striped tie. His receding dark hair was combed straight back severely and as usual made him appear as if he'd recently stepped from a shower. Canby remembered the Thorpe of twenty years and fifty pounds ago who'd been an arrogantly handsome man who could charm both wealthy matrons and streetwalkers.

"Hello, Les," Canby said. Thorpe hated to be called by his actual given name, Elias.

Thorpe smiled and they shook hands. "I hope you're rested from your vacation, Dex."

"Seems I came back with perfect timing." Canby sat down behind his desk and watched Thorpe sit in one of the high-backed wood chairs.

"I've never seen anything as bad as the Morgell Trust scene," Canby said. For him, the events of yesterday and last night had taken on the detachment of a remembered dream. Thorpe was here to remind him that it had all been real.

"So far it's 467 dead, 1138 injured." Thorpe's jowly face was somber. "We're still counting."

Canby felt a dropping sensation in his stomach as he tried to comprehend the significance of those figures, multiplied them by the average number of grieving relatives. How many children had been left with one parent or been orphaned? He pushed this sort of maudlin thinking to an unfeeling corner of his mind; it served only to get in the way of his job. And as far as Canby was concerned, his job in relation to the Morgell Trust disaster was for the main part ended.

He had pushed the door to within a few inches of its frame when he had entered the office and seen Thorpe. The oddly soothing crackling voice of the dispatcher wafted unintelligibly into the room, then was drowned out by louder voices from the booking desk. A suspect was stating his case out of court, claiming in highly injured tones that something had been planted on his person by the arresting officers. Thorpe rose from his chair, closed the door the rest of the way and sat back down. Canby noticed for the first time that the commissioner was wearing glossy patent leather black dress shoes.

"The bomb squad's been over the scene at the Morgell wreckage," Thorpe said.

Canby wasn't surprised. That was the usual procedure. He watched Thorpe light a slender dark cigar and knew something more was coming.

Thorpe squinted at Canby over the glowing cigar tip as if he were a surveyor calculating boundaries. "The explosions were set off deliberately, Dex. Seven charges, probably dynamite, planted about the interior of the building's foundation." A curl of gray smoke emerged like a medium's ectoplasm from Thorpe's parted lips. He had been trying to blow a smoke ring but hadn't succeeded.

Canby's breath momentarily left him. H
something simple and accidental, maybe a t
tank explosion. But all along he'd known th
accidental explosion couldn't have been powe
bring down an entire forty-story building. And t
ing hadn't collapsed of its own accord had beer
The explosions about its foundation were bot
heard by countless witnesses.

"So now we can expect a letter," Canby said.

"Letter?"

"From whichever terrorist group is responsible—along with letters from whichever terrorist groups and/or crackpots want to claim responsibility. There'll be dozens of crank phone calls, too, but usually the real thing comes in the mail. That way it's something tangible and carries credibility."

"Maybe you're right about a terrorist group or a politically motivated bombing," Thorpe said, "but don't count on it." Another thick curl of smoke, a misshapen ring at best. "Interesting thing about this bombing. Did you notice how the wreckage was confined to such a small ground area?"

"I'm told the building came straight down."

"It did. It collapsed in on itself. That's the way vacant buildings slated for demolition in congested areas have been razed for the past ten or twelve years, Dex. Demolition experts plant charges at strategic points and the building 'implodes,' as they call it, collapses over a relatively small area about its base. It's the cheapest way to demolish a tall building, and the fastest."

Canby recalled seeing TV news accounts of buildings being demolished in such a manner. There was always a great deal of dust, smoke and noise, then handshakes all around as the demolition people congratulated each other on a successful operation. This time there had been people in the building and on the streets below. And maybe somewhere someone had congratulated someone else on the perfect vertical descent and complete destruction of the building. A spur of anger dug into Canby's stomach.

doubt we'll receive some of those letters you men-
ned," Thorpe said, "and that will give the FBI the needed
excuse to enter the case. Naturally, if that happens we cooperate fully. But at the same time we'll have an independent
department investigation of the crime, on a smaller but possibly more effective scale. You're in charge of that investigation, Dex."

Canby felt a creeping wariness. But after all, the explosion
had occurred in the seventeenth. It was the way the assignment was being presented to him that made him uneasy.

"I recommended you," Thorpe said. It was far from a secret
that his position as commissioner wasn't as secure as it might
have been. There were those close to the mayor who were
pushing for a police commissioner more "progressive."

"How much autonomy do I have?"

"As much as possible. I'll back you."

And share in the credit if the case is broken, Canby
thought. A colorful feather for any political cap. He didn't
blame Thorpe; that was the game. Canby stood to gain by
the maneuver also. But if the case remained unbroken . . .

"I know what you're thinking," Thorpe said with his wide,
familiar smile. "You're right. It's a plum or a lemon, depending on how things turn out."

"I couldn't have put it more clearly," Canby said, tilting
back in his swivel chair as if some pressure were being ex-
erted on his chest.

"I'm having the bomb squad report sent over to you when
it's ready," Thorpe said.

"Who was in charge?"

"Felstein."

"He's the best. I'll talk to him personally after I read the
report."

"Stay on this one heavy," Thorpe said. "Let somebody else
here handle the day-in, day-out stuff if it piles up."

"Mathews can do that." Lucky Mathews, Canby found
himself thinking. The young lieutenant hadn't yet reached
the stage of his career where politics mixed in. Or had he?

"Life is politics," somebody famous had once said.

Thorpe was standing. The expression on his expansive, smiling features indicated that business was concluded. "How was the fishing?"

"Not good. My luck's going to have to turn around."

They shook hands again. Thorpe's smile faded to his characteristic near-angry expression. His inlaid diamond ring cut into Canby's finger.

"Keep me apprised," Thorpe said.

"I will, Les."

Canby watched the bulky, elegantly attired figure leave his office, trailing a lingering thread of cigar smoke. Throughout both men's careers, Thorpe had handed Canby these two-edged swords. Usually they'd cut the right way, but there was always danger.

Canby was in civilian clothes. He loosened his tie and sat at his desk again to attack what he could of the routine paperwork requiring his signature.

Less than an hour later, Norris came in and handed him the bomb squad report on the Morgell Trust case.

The report was less than revealing. The seven explosive charges had been placed within the building's foundation. They had been set at critical points so that the building's supporting structure would be suddenly removed, the exterior walls would fall in toward each other and the effect would be intensified as the building collapsed. The job had to have been done by an expert. For the building to be brought straight down, the charges had to explode almost simultaneously and with precise force. Almost certainly they had been detonated by a common electrical charge. Such a charge could be triggered by an electronic signal.

Canby phoned Central and asked Felstein to come over and talk with him. Felstein said he could be there in twenty minutes.

As Canby replaced the receiver, Molly Garrity knocked, then entered. She was a small woman in her early forties, red-haired but with that vanilla-translucent complexion with which only a few redheads are endowed. A civilian employee, she was wearing a neatly tailored brown pants suit that subtly emphasized the grace of her slender frame. Her face was symmetrical and small-featured, with sensitive, pliant lips, a winsome trace of freckles across the bridge of her straight nose and green eyes uptilted at the outer corners. She was eye-catching rather than conventionally pretty, but as one got to know her, her beauty seemed to increase and had a cumulative effect.

"I hear you had quite a night," she said.

Canby stood, walked to her, and they kissed lightly, a business-hours kiss.

"Not the kind of night I envisioned," Canby said. He saw that Molly was holding several papers in her right hand.

"I thought I'd bring these to you myself," she said, following his gaze to the papers. "It gave me an excuse to see you. They're letters, one addressed here, the other to Central."

"Nothing to the newspapers yet?"

"If they received any, they're still sitting on them. But give it time, it's still early." She handed him the letters and their accompanying envelopes as if reluctantly bestowing a gift.

Both letters were on inexpensive and common stationery practically impossible to trace. It was possible that the lab might bring out some fingerprints with ninhydrin, but not at all likely. One letter was crudely printed with a felt-tipped pen, explaining that the Morgell Trust Building had been destroyed as a warning to rich capitalist exploiters that the Third World was prepared to strike back. It was signed by an organization calling itself "Militants for the Millions."

The second letter was unsigned, composed of words carefully scissored out of a newspaper and applied with paste. It maintained that the building had been leveled and its occupants killed as a message from God to the effect that sin had gotten out of hand.

But that's been true for some time, Canby thought as he set the letters and envelopes on his desk corner. He would have them run over to the lab later and gather what information he could on "Militants for the Millions," if there actually was such an organization.

After any tragic occurrence it was common to receive such messages from the marginally sane. Some of these people, Canby knew, would convince themselves of their responsibility for the disaster and actually be able to pass a polygraph test.

"I've been chosen to press the Morgell Trust investigation," he told Molly.

"I know. I came to offer my help when and if you need it. Something as terrible as what happened . . . whoever did it *has* to be caught!"

"I'll need your help," Canby said, and watched the flesh at the corners of Molly's green eyes crinkle in fine concert with her smile.

He had thought until six months ago that he was too emptied to feel about a woman as he felt about Molly. And Bernice's memory still walked his mind, even after so much time had passed since her death from Hodgkin's disease. Their daughter Kara was grown and attending college in Mexico City, so Canby had borne the brunt of the hardship and grief. Talking to Molly had exorcised much of his debilitating remorse and empty loneliness. Molly and hard work had been his salvation.

"Dinner tonight?" Canby said.

"If you have time." She was half joking with him. "You know I hate to cook."

"There'll be time."

But Canby knew she'd understand if they couldn't keep their dinner date. Understanding was her rare gift.

Norris buzzed on the intercom to tell Canby that Felstein from the bomb squad had arrived. Molly left the office, and Canby told Norris to have Felstein come in.

Al Felstein was a small, handsome man with steady dark eyes and manicured, tapered fingers. His mannerisms were relaxed and subdued. There was nothing about him to suggest that he had the courage, expertise and nerves to disarm over a dozen planted explosive devices during the past three years.

"Captain," he said simply, by way of greeting, and with a smile settled into a chair near the desk. He and Canby had worked together a few times before.

Canby returned the smile. "Morgell Trust," he said, and the smile was gone. "You got there too late to do anything about that one, didn't you, Al."

"Those are the kind we can't do anything about, except work to prevent the next one."

"Anything off the record?"

Felstein shrugged, motioned with a graceful, almost feminine hand that reminded Canby of a Michelangelo painting. "It's all pretty much in the report. We didn't recover any fragments of the explosives' casings; there wasn't much chance in all that mess."

"The work of one man?"

"Could be. No way to know for sure."

"What do you feel?"

"I feel it probably was one man. This had to be done expertly, Captain. One man was perfectly capable of the job, and there aren't all that many demolition experts who specialize in razing buildings in that manner." Felstein's dark eyes brightened for an instant. "And maybe it would be unlikely for two people to get together who both had that much murder in them."

"Don't count on that, Al. How long would it take to plant the charges?"

"Twenty minutes maybe. With good planning, everything prepared. They didn't have to be particularly powerful charges; it was more a matter of where and how they were placed. And whoever placed them knew his work."

"So we look for a professional demolition man who's worked razing tall buildings in congested areas?"

"It'd be the place to dig in, sir."

When Felstein had gone, Canby called in Mathews and

34

instructed him to contact all the demolition companies in the area and get the names of anyone either employed by them or simply known by them who might have the expertise to have planted the type of charges that destroyed the Morgell Trust Building. Then Canby asked for a list of survivors who were inside or near the building at the time of the explosions. Probably there would be little to learn from them, but there always might be some small, seemingly insignificant piece of information that could lead to something crucial. The initial probing in such a case, the groping for a handle, was the most frustrating phase.

There was little else Canby could do until Mathews supplied him with the needed information.

The temperature outside had climbed to near ninety, and Canby suddenly noticed that his bare forearms were slippery with perspiration against the wood desk top. He swiveled in his chair, stretched his body and reached out to rotate the dial of the already laboring window air conditioner to high. The abrupt increased rush of air was pleasantly cold along his arm and damp shirt-sleeve.

Canby decided to do what was necessary to keep his dinner date with Molly that evening. Soon enough he'd be too busy to plan his personal life even a few hours ahead.

5

David Strother was late.

Not that he was due at a particular time at the offices of Doyle, Rogers and White Architectural Services, but it was understood that employees even of Strother's status were to be on the premises by nine-thirty each weekday morning.

This morning Strother had overslept. He had been awake until almost 3 A.M., his subconscious fencing restlessly with thrusts of doubt and unreasonable guilt. Finally he'd gotten up and was actually intending to go outside for a walk. Then, fully dressed except for his untied shoes, he'd fallen asleep sitting on the sofa in his apartment living room. And that was where he'd awakened, slumped sideways with one foot on the floor, at nine-forty this morning.

Considering what had happened, it wasn't likely that his tardiness would go unnoticed. But he had hopes.

His mind still sleep-fuzzed, his stomach reminding him he'd forgotten about breakfast, Strother pushed his way through glass double doors and crossed the checkerboard-tiled lobby to the elevators. He pressed the up button, folded his hands in front of him and stood patiently waiting.

Strother was a tall, long-limbed man of thirty-five, with unruly curly brown hair cut to just below the collar, a lean, chiseled sort of chin and a wide, serious mouth. He'd have been macho TV commercial-handsome but for amiable, curious blue eyes behind clear-framed glasses that lent him an indoors, vaguely owlish expression. The stylish cut of his vested blue suit and the habitual erectness of his carriage negated some of last night's effects on his appearance. But there was a darkness beneath his eyes and a tight downturn at the corners of his mouth.

The elevator arrived. A delivery man with a large cardboard carton he could barely manage staggered out, and Strother stepped in and pressed the button for the eleventh floor, where his office was located.

Strother walked across thick powder-blue carpet, nodded hello to Maggie the receptionist and turned down the hall leading to his office. Ellen Kane, the secretary he shared with Frank Benham, was seated typing at her cluttered semi-circular desk. She peeked like an in-season animal from behind a tall vase of flowers at Strother and said, "Doyle wants to see you."

Not "Mr. Doyle," Strother noted. Trouble. Ellen had ways of letting him know. She was absorbed again in her work, playing the typewriter keys with the intense concentration of a Horowitz at the piano.

Strother nodded wordlessly though he knew she wouldn't see him, entered his office, took a perfunctory glance through his mail, then walked out again past Ellen and toward Victor Doyle's office.

Doyle had him sent in immediately.

The office was large and airy, furnished with a decorator's touch, more for appearances than for efficiency. Victor Doyle, one of the company's founders, stood up from behind his massive antique desk and smiled at Strother. Doyle was a kindly-appearing man in his late sixties, wearing his invariable

37

gray pinstripe suit and cockeyed bow tie. He had full, ruddy cheeks and narrow dark eyes. A fringe of long white hair combed over his ears gave him the look of a prankish, prematurely aged third grader.

"David," he said, "we wondered when you'd turn up."

"I wasn't feeling too well this morning."

Concern crossed Doyle's cherubic face. "You're over whatever it was, I hope."

"I think so, sir."

"Fine." The smile came back on. "In here, please, David." Doyle motioned elegantly toward the small conference room off his office.

Strother expected to find someone else in the conference room, but it was empty, a simple, pleasant room with a wide window and a wider gleaming walnut conference table surrounded by eight comfortable chairs upholstered in royal blue. The room seemed cooler than the rest of the building.

Doyle sat in the chair at the head of the bare table, and Strother sat in a chair at the side of the table, to the left of Doyle. Strother had little doubt as to the subject of their conversation. Doyle, Rogers and White Architectural Services had been the designers and, through a subsidiary subcontracting firm, the builders of the Morgell Trust Building.

The Morgell Trust job had been one of the most ambitious that Doyle, Rogers and White had ever undertaken. And in fact the company had been in mild financial difficulty when it contracted for the job with Morgell. At that time there had been whispered rumors about kickbacks, but Strother was sure none of the rumors were true. Doyle, Rogers and White simply had submitted the best and most economical design. Of course Strother was somewhat prejudiced, as he was the architect of record who had for the most part designed the Morgell Trust Building.

"As you know, I'm a man who generally speaks directly to the point," Doyle was saying, "but this time I confess I find it difficult."

Strother could smell the lingering scent of cigar smoke in

the conference room. Doyle didn't smoke.

"If it makes it easier for you, sir," Strother said, "I'd prefer that we got immediately to the point."

Doyle unconsciously worked his lips as if there were an unpleasant taste in his mouth. "After much and painful discussion during the past few days, David, it's been decided that it would be in the best interest of the company if you were to resign."

Strother felt the soft blue upholstery press against his shoulder blades. He hadn't expected *this.* "Who made this decision?"

"The board of directors. We took a vote, David."

"And I suppose it was unanimous."

"No, there was one dissenter. Me. That's why I volunteered to talk with you."

"I can't say that I follow that logic."

"No one *wants* this, David. But the board decided that it was the wisest course."

"Why?"

Doyle stood up and walked to the wide window, and Strother turned in his chair to watch him. Against the harsh morning light, Doyle appeared peculiarly old and wasted. He was working his lips again.

"David, there are those who think the Morgell Trust Building should have withstood the force of the explosions."

"But that's absurd! Those were carefully placed charges at the structure's load-bearing points. That building was imploded, made to collapse in on itself. It was razed with professional skill but with people inside."

"You and I know all that, David. The board knows it. It's some of our clients who've been posing questions. It's an unreasonable but not unexpected psychological reaction, like the factors that sometimes cause the stock market to plummet for no valid reason. But, David, we have a responsibility to see to it that our stock, so to speak, remains high."

"But not a responsibility to your employees?"

"It's a question of which is the greater responsibility."

39

"Or the most profitable."

"You're being unfair, David." Doyle moved out of the window's rectangle of harsh light. "Or perhaps you're not. Either way, I don't suppose I can blame you for feeling as you do."

"But it won't make any difference."

"It can't." Doyle returned to his chair but didn't sit down. He leaned forward slightly, bracing himself on the chair back with his frail hands. "You'll receive two months' severance pay, David."

"Am I supposed to consider that generous?"

"I'd hoped you'd understand, that's all. The entire matter is regrettable, tragic."

"But it requires a scapegoat."

"If you must think along those lines, think more in terms of a sacrificial lamb." Doyle's narrow shoulders lifted in a hopeless shrug. "Unfortunately, that's what life sometimes demands, David."

Strother stood up and buttoned his suit coat. "Right now, Mr. Doyle, the company's stock isn't very high on my exchange."

"I am sorry, David," Doyle said behind him, as Strother walked from the room.

After Strother had cleaned out his desk, he said good morning to a tearful Ellen and went back home to his apartment. It would take him several days of brief visits to the office to wrap up his roles in various projects. Now that he'd fully accepted the fact that his job was irrevocably terminated, he wished he could sever his ties with Doyle, Rogers and White completely and instantaneously, so that he wouldn't have to return there even for an hour or two. Walking out abruptly wasn't the way things were done, but now that he'd assimilated his initial disappointment, Strother was angry as well as disillusioned.

He crossed the living room and sat down on the low sofa, stared at without seeing the large, overstocked bookshelves on the opposite wall. The apartment was small, buff-colored, furnished in tones of beige and dark brown with touches of red. It was a twelfth-floor corner unit in a well-kept building just off Lexington Avenue. It was private. It was quiet. It was lonely.

What now?

For the first time in a long time, Strother had nothing, absolutely nothing, that he was obligated to do. He glanced at his wristwatch, then realized that the time didn't matter; there was no place he had to be. He felt suddenly frightened and isolated, cut off from much that was important in his life, and his anger again began to rise in ominous turmoil deep in the pit of his stomach. He stood and walked into the kitchen, poured three fingers of Chivas Regal scotch into a glass, then dropped in two ice cubes that crackled in short-lived protest.

By the time he'd returned to the living room and was sitting again on the sofa, drink in hand, he realized that some of his anger was directed at himself. As was some of his pity.

Unreasonable as it seemed, he did harbor a deep, guilty sense of responsibility for the horror of the Morgell Trust Building disaster.

Maybe it hadn't been such an expert demolition job; maybe the building should have withstood the force of the explosions. It took rare expertise to bring down such a massive structure with such precise and total destruction. Some buildings, because of design and internal structure, simply couldn't be destroyed efficiently in such a manner.

But many could. Why had the Morgell Trust Building, *his* building, been chosen?

There was the problem, Strother realized as he lifted the glass to his lips. He did see the Morgell Trust Building as his building, his handiwork and a measure of himself. That was simply how a good architect felt about his work. And now his building had been destroyed by a madman, an indiscriminate mass killer. And Strother, in his own special way, was one of the injured.

He sat working slowly on his drink, listening to the irregular rushing sounds of traffic from the street below, staring at the rolls of design paper on the drawing board he kept set up in the corner by the window. It wasn't even noon; it was too early to be drinking. He would have phoned Ann, but he knew she was on a job, photographing a morose bloodhound for a dog-food advertisement. He took another sip of scotch. The silence in the apartment seemed to pulsate in his ears.

He had to get out, go somewhere to be near people, noise, conversation. It was almost 11:30 A.M., so he decided to leave the apartment and have an early lunch.

He walked along Lexington, among scurrying businessmen and tourists, panhandlers and high-powered hustlers. The rich and the poor. The close juxtaposition and startling contrast of wealth and poverty was one of the features of Manhattan that had always fascinated him. It seemed a volatile chemistry that somehow never exploded, only fermented.

Twenty minutes later Strother sat at a window table in a Beer 'n' Burger restaurant, watching pedestrians stream by on the other side of the rain-spotted glass. He sipped a cold stein of beer as he waited for his Gardenburger plate. There was noise here, the muted conversation of the other customers, occasional taunting in Spanish from the kitchen, a friendly argument on the other side of the arched doorway leading to the small, dim bar. The dark-haired waitress who brought Strother's hamburger and oversized salad smiled at him with crooked but very white teeth and said she hoped he'd enjoy his lunch.

Though the food was fine, Strother didn't enjoy it. He ate slowly and mechanically, chewing each bite as if it might somehow be harmful unless thoroughly pulverized. All the while he ate he stared absently out the window, at the bustling traffic and the swarms of hurrying employees on their way to lunch.

When he finished his hamburger and turned from the window, Strother saw that a customer who'd been seated near him had left a morning *Times* folded on the seat of a chair. He saw the bold black letters "RGELL" and, still in a semi-

42

seated position, left his chair, took a long step and returned to his table with the newspaper.

Strother saw nothing new in the paper. There was a photograph of the Morgell Trust Building, taken shortly before the destruction, and an updated list of the disaster's victims. Strother didn't look at the four columns of names and addresses; he didn't want to know how many more bodies had been found in the mass of rubble.

As his eyes avoided the list of victims, Strother read that someone named Captain Dexter P. Canby was in charge of the investigation into the Morgell Trust bombing. There was an account of a small impromptu press conference: "Is there any doubt that the building's destruction was a criminal act rather than an accident?" a reporter had asked Canby. "There is no doubt whatsoever," Canby had replied. Another member of the press had asked, "Why exactly have you been put in charge of the investigation, Captain?" Canby: "The crime was committed within my jurisdiction." Press: "Do you think you're close to solving the crime?" Canby: "There are avenues of investigation we're exploring." Press: "Are there any suspects at this time?" Canby neither hedged nor was evasive in his answer.

"No," he said.

6

1974

"In the interest of healing and mercy, he pardoned him!" the husky, dark-haired man said in an annoyed tone, his voice muffled by the mouthful of toast he was chewing.

"Who did what?" the woman on the other side of the table asked, pouring milk onto her fortified cornflakes.

"Ford! He pardoned Nixon yesterday." The man washed down the toast with a gulp of coffee that was too hot and burned his tongue.

He was an impatient man in the small things, a tirelessly patient man in the large. And he was a willful man—willful in a way not to be confused with merely stubborn. In his dark features and his deep-set brown eyes was stamped the mark of a man who had rare energies on which to draw. A driven man who had almost but not quite tamed his personal demons. Of all things about him, the woman loved him most for his willfulness.

"I didn't think you could pardon someone who hadn't been convicted," she said, replacing the milk in the refrigerator

44

and sitting down across from her husband at the small table.

He snorted, flipped a page of the paper. "With power and money, you can step off the game board and play by your own rules."

The woman, a small, sedately pretty brunette, hesitated before commenting. "Aren't we setting up our own rules?"

"Exactly. Just as they do. But with as much risk as they can make possible for us. And it was them, not us, who changed the game." He looked closely at her, as if searching for some flaw in priceless artwork. "Do you still have qualms?"

She couldn't quite read the dark message in his eyes. "You know I do," she said in her imperturbable melodic voice. "Several qualms. But mostly I'm afraid of being caught."

"Always a chance," he conceded. She'd been honest with him. "But even less chance than our ex-President had of being found out."

From outside the kitchen's open window came the sounds of the street, the wavering hum of passing cars, children shouting in mock—or real?—desperation.

"How many buildings now?" the woman asked her husband, taking a bite of stale and soggy cornflakes. Not enough sugar.

"Five," he said. He watched her sprinkle sugar evenly over her cereal. She was so effortlessly precise in everything she did.

"Isn't five enough?" she asked.

He shook his head no. "When the time comes, there should be as many as possible. Their number will determine our actual strength. We'll continue with the plan we've followed from the beginning."

She nodded. She pitied anyone who stood in the path of her husband in pursuit of his goal. He was a force to be avoided when he'd set his mind and begun executing the details of his dreams.

A warm breeze pushed its way in through the open window and played over the checkered tablecloth, moving one draped corner gently against the woman's leg. She found herself wondering if her husband would be as he was if they were able to have children. If *she* were able.

But her wondering was pointless: it was impossible for her to give birth. When she was sixteen, she had found herself involved with an older, very wealthy man. His wife was a customer of the sixteen-year-old girl's mother, who was a seamstress. And one day when the daughter went to the man's apartment in the East Sixties to deliver a dress, the man explained that his wife was away but would be back soon. Would the girl wait so the wife could try on the dress?

She did wait, too shy to refuse. And she didn't refuse a small glass of wine that had contained something more than wine. Or had it? She still wasn't sure; she preferred to think it had.

The man's wife had left him permanently, but the girl hadn't found that out until well into the night. Still, that seemed to make what had happened, and the gift of a bracelet and a gold pendant, more acceptable. She was easily convinced to stay until morning.

Three months later, it all changed when she told the man she was pregnant. Time for naïveté and youth-nurtured hopes to be destroyed. Time for an abortion at the hands of a doctor who also accepted money to see to it that she would be sterile.

After the abortion, the man explained that he'd arranged for her never to have that problem again. As if he'd done her a favor. He was actually surprised when she left him for good.

A long time ago. Her husband knew all about it. Telling him, before their marriage, had been difficult for her.

She finished her cornflakes.

Her husband had listened, had understood and was patient with her.

7

The Present

Norris's voice came neutral and guarded over the intercom in Canby's office. "There's a man here at the desk who wants to talk to you about the Morgell Trust case, Captain. He says his name's Strother."

Canby was vaguely annoyed as he punched the intercom button. "Has Mathews talked to him?"

"He won't see Mathews, sir, he demands to see you."

One of the disadvantages of having your name in the newspapers in connection with a sensational case, Canby mused unhappily. Suddenly you were the object of attention of most of the city's crackpots and amateur sleuths. He didn't feel like talking to someone who might not be rational, yet he couldn't turn down any potential lead. And Norris wouldn't have announced the man's request to see Canby unless he'd sensed with a veteran cop's intuition that something might come of it.

"Send him in," Canby said.

A few seconds later a tall, intensely owlish-looking man

entered the office. He was carrying a long cardboard tube.

"I'm David Strother, Captain Canby." As he spoke, he shifted the cardboard tube so he could shake hands with Canby. He had the deceptively powerful talonlike grip of many slender men.

Canby motioned for Strother to sit down and lowered himself again into his desk chair. "I understand you have information about yesterday's Morgell Trust bombing," he said.

"In a sense, yes. But what I really came for was to find out what you know. And to offer my personal services."

"I'm frankly more interested in your information than in your services," Canby said. He was beginning to suspect he was dealing with someone he should never have let enter. Despite Norris's talent for sensing the genuine thing, perhaps the importance of the case had swayed him.

"But I want to help." There was a flash of desperation in the owlish blue eyes. And something else, possibly dangerous.

Canby was about to stand and begin politely easing Strother from the office. He shifted forward in his desk chair.

"I know exactly where the explosive charges were planted," Strother said.

Canby doubted that, but he relaxed and waited patiently for Strother to continue.

"They were planted at supporting beams and at the building's stress points," Strother said, "then detonated at precisely the right times and with precisely the correct force to bring the building in on itself. It had to be done by an expert demolition man schooled and experienced in the method."

"We're compiling a list of those explosives experts now."

"I've already talked to one," Strother said.

To Canby's surprise, Strother stood and drew a rolled sheet of white-etched blue paper from the long cardboard tube. He walked over and spread the paper on Canby's desk.

"This is a blueprint of the Morgell Trust Building," he said, "basement through fourth floor. From the fourth story up, the floors are almost identical."

Canby stood and stared down carefully at the blueprint.

48

It appeared genuine. He weighted opposite edges of the taut paper with an ashtray and the base of his desk phone. "Where did you get this?"

Strother raised an arched eyebrow in mild surprise. "Didn't I tell you? I'm the architect who designed the Morgell Trust Building." He bowed his head to look again at the spread, curled blueprint. "The red circles are the points where the charges had to have been placed for that type of damage to occur. The numbers beneath the circles are the strength of the respective charges, measured in sticks of dynamite. Of course, dynamite sticks weren't necessarily used. Packed blasting powder or canisters are just as likely." He pulled another blueprint from beneath the first and spread it out. "This is a side view; you can see what happens if these"—Strother's forefinger darted from point to point on the paper—"and these are suddenly removed. These walls collapse. A domino effect is created, moving upward floor by floor as the building drops straight down into its own rubble." His hand slapped flatly against the paper.

"Who was the explosives man who gave you this information?" Canby asked.

"Gordon Egger of Hannah Wrecking Company. He told me what it would take in explosive force and explained precisely where the blast points would be. Egger's worked for Hannah Wrecking for years, and he's razed more than a few condemned buildings using the same technique."

Canby made a note of Egger's name and employer. He could cross-check the information later with Mathews' list. "Can you leave me these blueprints?" he asked Strother.

"I can give you copies. If you have a copy machine, we can run them off here."

"We have one upstairs." Canby pressed his intercom button and asked Norris to send in the clerk. He leaned back away from the blueprints, which Strother released from the ashtray and telephone and let flip back into a neat roll. "I can understand your desire to help, Mr. Strother, but there was no need to talk with a demolition man before we did.

It might have impeded the investigation. Not that I don't appreciate your interest, but how come so much concern?"

Strother sat back down, his lean, long-fingered hands clutching his knees as if he were trying to wring his kneecaps. "I lost my livelihood and my reputation because of that building's destruction, Captain."

"Why?"

"Because when something like that happens in my business, I suppose somebody's got to accept the blame. At least that's what they tell me. Some of the clients of my former employer believe the building should have withstood the force of the explosions."

"Could it have?"

"Not according to Gordon Egger."

"But you don't believe him."

"I believe him. But Egger has no way of knowing if the charges were set by someone as expert in the job as he is."

"They had to have been, if the building came down. Whoever planted the charges must have done just about what Egger would have done." Canby wondered what he was doing in this hoop-snake conversation.

"I know that, Captain, but I don't feel it. I feel . . . somehow responsible."

"On the face of it, Mr. Strother, that seems like self-flagellation."

Strother appeared thoughtful, chewed his lower lip and nodded. "There's more, Captain. You have to understand how an architect might feel about having created something like the Morgell Trust Building. The great satisfaction of the job is in the responsibility for the mass, line and balance of the structure. And if I'm qualified to accept that kind of responsibility, then I must in a sense accept responsibility for the building's fate, at least a fate like the Morgell Trust Building's. In a very real way, beyond deeds and ownership, that building was mine, a part of me, and someone destroyed it."

"That, Mr. Strother, is an emotional and unfortunate way to view the situation."

50

"But an unavoidable way in my case. That's why I'd like to help you personally in whatever way I can, because the destruction of the building is a destruction I take very personally."

Canby didn't doubt the sincerity of Strother's words. The young architect was leaning forward in his chair, his long face lined with earnestness and a need to have Canby understand. Canby tried.

Youth, he thought, with some distaste and a relief at having passed that passion-ruled period of his life. For a brief while, long ago, Canby had studied art, been a serious painter in oils. He knew how he'd have felt if someone had destroyed one of his canvases. And in every way they were of lesser dimension than the Morgell Trust Building. Canby sighed, stared at the distraught young man across the desk from him.

"What do you mean by 'help'?" he asked.

"I . . . really don't know. I suppose I could be something of a technical consultant. Not that I couldn't help in other ways . . ."

The clerk, a pubescent-looking probationary patrolman, came in and got the blueprints.

"We have men for legwork," Canby said, when the clerk had left.

"But never enough. And since I'm going to be out there doing what you call legwork anyway, it might as well be under your unofficial direction."

"Unofficial?"

"I understand I'm just an ordinary citizen without police powers, Captain."

Canby had seen such police-civilian alliances of convenience before. "But could you continue to understand that, Mr. Strother?"

"It's David, Captain."

"Then answer the question, David."

"Yes. I could always bear in mind my limitations. I'm not asking a great deal, Captain, only to be around and useful."

Canby didn't want to turn Strother down flat; there might

be much to gain by nurturing his cooperation. But what Strother was suggesting could backfire in ways the architect didn't suspect. For a long time Canby sat listening to the muted crackling litany of the police dispatcher and from far away outside the fading high note of a siren reverberating among the tall buildings. He stared unabashedly at Strother.

There was a knock on the door, and the clerk returned with the copies and originals of the blueprints. When he'd gone, Canby said, "Let me think about it, David."

Strother nodded slowly and unsteadily, as if the weight of his head were suddenly too much for the strength of his neck. "That's fair, Captain." He drew a small notebook from his shirt pocket and jotted down his name, address and phone number, then with a flourish tore out the sheet of paper with the information and laid it on Canby's desk. "For when you make up your mind," he said, smiling. Canby noted that he had the sort of smile women called disarming.

Canby stood up and they shook hands again. Strother was slipping the rolled blueprints back into their cardboard tube as he left the office.

Seated back behind his desk, Canby idly began to tap a foot rhythmically on the hard floor, as if keeping time to some measured, hectic musical composition. Life had thrown another disturbing possibility at him, another choice. No matter how effective and professional his investigation, he knew that in some matters there could really be no substitute for the specialized expertise of someone like Strother. Expertise coupled with strong motivation. But perhaps a motivation that was too strong.

Canby decided that dealing with David Strother could be a troublesome matter. And Canby sidestepped trouble whenever he could, reasoning that there was enough trouble in life that couldn't be avoided.

8

In the cheery, sun-lanced dining room of the mayor's Upper East Side mansion, Mayor William Danner sat at the small corner table near a window that looked out over the well-tended garden. Neatly pruned privet hedges formed high, lush green walls. A curved flagstone walk from the French windows led down through rows of azaleas to a tiny pond stocked with goldfish. In the center of the pond was a small fountain, a perpetually tipped stone urn atop a graceful pillar. From where he sat Mayor Danner could hear its faint gurgling and splashing.

William Danner was a large man, a onetime football tailback for Fordham University. At fifty-six he was still flat-bellied and in sound physical condition. His hair was almost completely gray, combed to one side in an exaggerated fashion that drew gazes to the bald spot it was intended to conceal. Danner had an Irish brawler's good-humored, twinkling blue eyes and slightly pug, off-center nose, and he had a Scotch accountant's thin-lipped, calculating mouth and receding chin. But when he smiled, he was all Irish. The voters liked that and had elected him by a wide margin.

On the white tablecloth in front of him were a delicate china cup filled with steaming black coffee, a glass carafe containing more coffee, a silver setting and a tall glass of fresh-squeezed orange juice. To his right, on the table's near corner, was his personal morning mail, a stack of letters three or four inches high laid catercornered on a large brown envelope. It was Mayor Danner's custom to read through his mail each morning at breakfast.

The mayor downed his orange juice in two hearty tilts of the glass, then took a sip of coffee. Ellie, his maid, entered the dining area just then carrying his poached egg, toast and two slices of bacon on a round silver tray. The scent of the bacon put an edge on Danner's appetite.

Ellie was a square-shouldered, ageless woman who had been a maid for the city's mayors for more than a decade. She had the facility for getting along with whichever political personality occupied City Hall. And there was always, underlying the employer-employee relationship, the unspoken knowledge that Ellie was more firmly ensconced in her position than was the man she served in his.

She set the plate containing Danner's breakfast before him and turned to leave, adjusting the tight knot of white hair at the back of her head.

Danner probed at the poached egg with his fork. "This egg's not done, Ellie," he said. "How's a man supposed to cope with the problems of a thriving metropolis after eating an egg that isn't done?"

Ellie walked back and loomed over Danner, peering down at the egg. "Poached eggs are supposed to be soft."

"There's soft and there's soft, Ellie."

"There is, sir. And this egg is soft. How's the coffee?"

"Delicious as always."

"That's good, sir. Beautiful morning."

Danner agreed and glanced out the window, his attention

caught by a splash of bright blue, a small jay pecking and worrying at a maple branch. The jay flew away in a darting arc, and Danner turned to find that Ellie had left. He picked up his fork again and began to eat his egg.

After breakfast, he poured a second cup of coffee from the carafe, pushed his plate away and reached for the stack of mail. He drew from his pocket a small pearl-handled penknife and slit the flap of the large brown envelope. He was disappointed to find that it contained a glossy invitation to a fund-raising dinner. It occurred to him that substantial funds would have to be raised to pay for the printing of the invitations. He continued with the rest of the mail, setting aside those letters that required an answer.

With only two letters remaining, he opened the envelope that was to begin his political and personal ordeal.

The letter was printed with blue ink on a flimsy sheet of cheap typing paper. The printing was so uniform and symmetrical that it had to have been done with the aid of a ruler. Accompanying the letter was another, smaller sheet of paper on which was a penciled diagram that appeared to be a floor plan. Scattered about the diagram were several *X*s in the same blue ink that was used to print the letter. Mayor Danner read the letter once quickly then again very slowly.

Your Honor:

I am the one that destroyed the Morgell Trust Building and have the power to do more. For many years while buildings were under construction or remodeling I planted explosives inside them and have been waiting for the rite time. I can destroy hafe the city and will if you don't follow my instructions that I will get to you soon. If in three days you aren't reddy to pay me one million dollars in cash another building will be destroyed, and one will be destroyed every day until you do pay. You can try to find some of the buildings that carry my seed of death and might but you won't have enough time

55

to find them all or even a few. You have no choice but to pay, but God help you if you dont.

Jericho

Mayor Danner stared at the letter, trying to make himself believe it was the work of a harmless crackpot. But a cold premonition writhed at the back of his mind. He was sure the penciled diagram was supposed to constitute proof of some sort that the letter was genuine. His guess was that it represented the basement of the Morgell Trust Building. For the first time he examined the envelope closely. It was addressed in the same exact printing as the letter and carried a nine A.M. midtown postmark dated yesterday.

Then the mayor remembered that Jericho was the biblical city whose walls were brought down by Joshua using mighty trumpet blasts.

Danner placed the envelope back on the table, alongside the letter. Outside the window, the jay had returned and was chattering stridently. The sound irritated Danner. Still staring at the letter, he pushed back his chair and stood. He dabbed at his lips with his napkin, then laid the napkin by his plate and walked across the room to the small alcove that contained a telephone.

He dialed the private number of Commissioner Thorpe, who in turn phoned Captain Dexter P. Canby.

9

Canby stared down at the letter on his desk. Both the letter and the diagram Mayor Danner had received were lying atop a copy of the blueprint Strother had shown Canby. Despite pressures to the contrary, even Molly's cautious but persistent opinion that Militants for the Millions was to be taken seriously, Canby was sure now that he was staring at the real thing. The realization went beyond logic to an eerie coolness at the nape of his neck.

There was indeed an organization calling itself Militants for the Millions, a hang-on radical group that had its roots in the violent upheaval of the sixties. But all indications were that the group had been disbanded for the past several years, and it had never been its members' style to engage in the sort of violence that might claim human life. Canby's investigation had revealed that the most violent act for which the organization had been responsible was the hurling of bottles of blood into half a dozen local draft board offices. Five years ago there'd been rumors about the group's involvement in the planting of a bomb in an uptown bank, but only rumors. The bomb hadn't exploded, and fingerprints on the clockwork led to the eventual arrest and conviction of an extortionist wanted by the FBI. And the paper and neat printing that Canby was now staring at showed no similarity to the letter that was supposedly from Militants for the Millions.

The window air conditioner behind Canby began the high-pitched warbling sound that it now periodically made, no doubt the symptom of some malady that would leave Canby sweltering while waiting for it to be repaired. He hesitated to report the sound, especially now that he'd learned how to deal with it. He walked to the squealing air conditioner and slapped it sharply on the side with the heel of his hand. The warbling stopped and the air conditioner hummed smoothly, but Canby knew his method of stopping the sound was only a temporary measure.

There was a knocking on his door that he hadn't heard above the air conditioner's squeal. That would be Strother. Norris had been instructed to give him access. Canby called for him to enter.

"You made good time," Canby said, when Strother had closed the door behind him. "I phoned you only fifteen minutes ago."

Strother appeared tired. He had the haggard, gravity-afflicted look of a man who had not had nearly enough sleep. Dark crescents of flesh beneath his eyes gave the lenses of his glasses a burlesque bifocal look. "I don't live all that far away," he said.

"Another bad night?"

"They're not getting better, only longer."

For an instant Canby felt a deep sympathy for the guilt-plagued figure before him. Whether or not the responsibility for the Morgell Trust disaster was genuine, Strother felt it and was bending visibly beneath the burden. Canby picked up the letter the mayor had received and slipped it into his pocket before motioning for Strother to step over to the desk.

"Look at this," he said, tapping a forefinger on the penciled diagram with its blue *X*s, "and tell me what you make of it."

Strother supported himself with one hand on the desk as he leaned forward to peer down at the diagram, moved it aside to look more closely at the blueprint copy. "It's a floor plan of the Morgell Trust Building's basement."

"I knew that. But do you see any significant difference I might be overlooking? Might there be other buildings similar enough for this to be the floor plan of their basements?"

"No." Strother shook his head decisively, a lock of his curly hair dropping down over his forehead like a pouncing insect. "It's almost exact, even scaled to near the precise proportions."

"Almost exact?"

"It doesn't include some minor changes and an interior wall that was added later."

"So it might have been made when the building was under construction?"

"In its early stages, yes."

"Do you think someone familiar with architecture or the construction business drew this diagram?"

"I'd say so." Strother nodded in confirmation. "It shows some professional touches."

"The penned-in *X*s correspond with your markings on the blueprint to indicate where the explosive charges had to have been placed."

"I noticed that. They correspond perfectly."

Canby walked to the side of the desk so he could be facing Strother. "Would an explosives expert be able to draw such a diagram?"

"Sure. One who specializes in the kind of work we're talking about. It takes planning; it's constructive engineering in reverse."

"You mean he'd have to be a structural engineer?"

"No, but he'd need an engineer's knowledge concerning his own narrow field. The men who do this kind of work have that knowledge."

From beneath the blueprint copy Canby drew a sheet of

yellow paper. "This is a list of demolition men specializing in that type of work. Most are still working in the area, but some have left or retired, and a few have died. Do you know any of them?" He handed the paper to Strother, who straightened, turned so the light from the window was over his shoulder and studied the list.

The department computer had spat out the names after being fed spools of the information dug up by Mathews and his aides. There were fourteen names. The names and all information about them had been added to the computer bank along with the rest of the information so far accumulated on the Morgell Trust case. There was little for the computer to chew on. Canby couldn't remember the computer ever breaking a case, and he was sure it had never made an arrest.

"I recognized Egger's name, of course. I know him fairly well, and I've met Bert Taylor. Other than that I don't recognize any of the names. But I wouldn't. I only met Taylor once, through Egger."

Strother brushed back his hair, didn't seem to notice when it fell back onto his forehead. Again Canby caught the agony and concern in his owlish eyes.

"What did your father do?" Canby asked.

Strother looked at him in surprise. "My father?"

"What did he do for a living?"

"He sold shoes. He's still alive, but he's retired. Why?"

"Maybe I want to know more about you. How did he put you through school to become an architect? Shoe salesmen don't usually get to be independently wealthy."

"My father isn't. I worked my way through school, doing everything from gardening to waiting tables."

"Was your family poor?"

"Not poor, no. Well, I don't know—poor's relative."

"Down to a point. The difference between steak and hamburger is negligible compared to the difference between hamburger and nothing."

"We always had hamburger."

Canby walked to the window and stared out. The glass

was dirty. They never washed the windows here. Through the gritty haze Canby could barely make out movement behind some of the windows in the building across the street. Wasn't that how people usually looked at each other, across a void, through a haze?

And that was the way Strother must be looked at, Canby thought. There were no other choices but to accept him that way or not at all. Canby realized that the Morgell Trust Building tragedy was something far beyond the usual structure into which ordinary chaos could be fitted so as to be made manageable. If the right thing were to be done, the rules could only be stretched so far and then they must be broken. Though he could defend the unusual step of enlisting Strother's help, he could not defend it within the rules. The hard choice that sooner or later every bureaucrat had to make.

Canby turned from the window. He'd made up his mind.

"There's so much at stake," he said, almost to himself. He tensed his jaw muscles as if the words he was about to speak would hurt coming out. "I'm going to stick my neck out, David, and if it turns out I've made a mistake, I'll personally wring yours."

Strother appeared puzzled, then smiled through his weariness.

Reaching into his rear pocket, Canby withdrew the mayor's letter. "This arrived in Mayor Danner's morning mail in the envelope that contained the diagram you just examined."

Strother held the letter daintily, as if afraid of smudging nonexistent fingerprints, and read. His lean face settled into firm, Lincolnesque lines and seemed to age beneath the tiredness. He handed the letter back to Canby.

"I hope you're taking this letter seriously," he said.

"We are. That was the purpose of whoever wrote it including the diagram, to set it apart from the usual crank mail. That's why I phoned you to come here." He watched Strother, pleased by the bafflement on the younger man's face. "Does something about the letter confuse you?"

61

"Its lack of literacy. It seems that whoever drew that diagram would have composed a different sort of letter. But of course I'm not taking into account the possibility of mental derangement. The 'Jericho' signature suggests that whoever wrote the letter might be a religious fanatic."

"I don't think we're dealing with someone irrational—not in the sense you mean by 'mental derangement.'" Canby moved over to stand by Strother and show him the letter. "Some of the misspellings and other grammatical errors are a bit too obvious. And notice the word 'don't' contains an apostrophe in the sixth line but none in the last."

"You mean whoever wrote this was attempting to appear semiliterate to mislead the police."

"Not entirely. The fashion this is written in is calculated more to disguise any clue to level of education and position, meant to be more of a smoke screen than an instrument to mislead in some particular direction."

"Do you see any clues despite the intent to disguise?"

"The syntax is deliberately garbled, but in line three, instead of 'being built,' we have 'under construction.' And notice that common words like 'right' and 'ready' are misspelled, but nothing that has to do with construction or demolition has been spelled wrong."

"Which substantiates the theory that we're dealing with somebody with intimate knowledge of the trade."

"I wouldn't say the letter substantiates the theory, but it's a strong indicator. And right now that theory is the only avenue of investigation that looks like anything but a dead end."

Strother walked to a chair by Canby's desk and sat down, sighing either in comfort or in perplexity. "How do you intend to proceed down that avenue?"

"We're going to locate every man on that list of demolition experts and interrogate them. You can help through your friend Egger. Get his opinions on whichever of these men he happens to know, find out their whereabouts. That might save us valuable time."

"Speaking of time," Strother said, "how long will it be

before that letter appears in the newspapers and on TV?"

"It won't be long. One of the most difficult parts of my job is avoiding reporters. And the mayor knows about the letter. He can't lie. None of us can afford to lie about something like this. All we can do is stay busy and hope for the best."

Strother stood and stretched his lean body. Lack of sleep had somehow lent him a hollow-chested, emaciated look. "Shall we start now?"

"You start with Egger," Canby told him. "I want to know all about him."

Strother grinned. "Do you trust anyone?"

"I trust you, David. Clock and calendar say I have to."

10

Mayor Danner had issued firm orders not to be disturbed for the next hour. He sat now in his office, behind the polished surface of his wide desk top, and looked incredulously at his chief administrative assistant, Carl Gaines.

Gaines was an unblinking man with a ruddy, square-chiseled face, well into his forties but with the lean, erect body of a thirty-year-old athlete beneath his conservative blue suit and vest. And indeed he did play racquetball every day, even on Sundays. He still had a full head of coarse brown hair, though now it was peppered with gray, but uniformly, as if even time respected Gaines' sense of order. He was an honest if devious man, with a genuine feeling of obligation to the public. He was also a decorated retired Air Force colonel, a former B-52 copilot in Vietnam, so perhaps Danner should have expected this.

"You can't mean what you're saying," Danner said.

Gaines locked steady fingers together on his blue-clad thigh and nodded calmly. "We have to refuse to pay the million dollars," he said. "To do otherwise will only encourage similar actions by similar extremists. In the long run, giving in will cost more lives."

"My tendency is to deal with the short run," Danner said, "and cope with the long run piece by piece as it comes at me. Carl, this isn't an abstract, hypothetical exercise. I have no real choice."

"I'm not a yes-man, Mr. Mayor. You asked for my opinion. I feel that you have no real choice but to refuse to cooperate with unknown maniacs who might well go ahead and do what they've threatened after receiving the money. We know they're capable. And there are plenty of people out there who'd kill at a dollar per life for a million dollars if they thought they could get away with it. And if you give in this time, they'll think so."

Mayor Danner wiped a hand down his face, dragging thumb and forefinger to distort the corners of his eyes. "Maybe you're right, Carl. But I have to act in accordance with my conscience."

Gaines didn't seem in the least offended. "Of course. You asked for my advice and got it, that's all. And no matter what you decide, I'll do everything I can to help."

"I know that, Carl." Danner rested an elbow on the glistening desk top and stared at the heavily draped window. There wasn't the slightest noise from outside; the large office was almost soundproof. "We do have three days," the mayor said. "I think you'll agree that for now, at least temporarily, we must cooperate."

"It would be sound strategy," Gaines admitted, but with a trace of reluctance. He drew a pack of Kools from his shirt pocket, placed one of the cigarettes between his thin lips and lit it with a small gold lighter. The lighter worked the first time, Danner noticed. Everything Gaines was associated with seemed to work with snap and precision. Aside from political considerations, it was why Danner had chosen Gaines as his chief aide.

Danner was beginning to wish, quite illogically, that he

hadn't consulted Gaines. Not that he wanted to be surrounded by aides who automatically assumed his perspective on problems—there were plenty of sycophants available—but he'd feel better about his dilemma if Gaines agreed with him at least in part. Not for the first time, Danner reflected that the high-ceilinged, paneled office, so formal, so hushed, was a lonely place from which to conduct the teeming city's business. But responsibility, real responsibility, carried with it its own peculiar loneliness. Danner had learned that long ago, but he hated to be reminded.

"I'll start raising the money," he said.

"Can you raise a million dollars soon enough?" Gaines asked. He drew on his cigarette as if he actually disliked smoking, and exhaled a thick cloud of grayish smoke as quickly as possible.

Danner nodded. "I've thought about that, Carl. It shouldn't be an insurmountable problem. I can't legally procure it from designated funds—at least not without attracting a great deal of attention that I don't want right now. But I can get the money from half a dozen banks. The city can guarantee repayment with interest."

Behind the grayish haze, Gaines seemed to be thinking. "The next move is the extortionists'," he said with slow consideration. "We'll have to receive instructions pertaining to the money's delivery."

"I expect that at any time."

"Why don't you tell them you're having trouble raising the money? Stall them as long as possible. We might have time to think of something."

"A dangerous game I have no right to play."

"A game it's your obligation to play. We shouldn't make it easy for them."

"You keep saying 'them.' "

"Them, him, her, whatever. The 'Jericho' epithet could mean anything. My instincts tell me something this big isn't a one-person operation."

"But we don't know," Danner said, anxiety tugging at the

66

corners of his mouth. "We don't know anything for sure . . ."

"We pray and wait," Gaines said. He was serious about the prayer. "Somewhere along the line we'll learn something more, and maybe you'll gain time and room to maneuver."

"Right now there's neither time nor room," Danner told him. "We're being kept in a tight corner and prodded."

"What about the news media?" Gaines asked.

"Stay unavailable."

Gaines smiled. "We agree on that."

Danner watched Gaines leave the office. When the heavy oak door had closed, he wondered what Gaines' reaction would be if cooperation were refused and thousands died. He'd never wondered such a thing about Gaines before.

He picked up the telephone, then replaced it on the desk corner. Would it be better to approach the bank officers individually or *en masse*? He decided after much finger-drumming to approach each bank on an individual basis, extracting a promise of confidentiality before revealing why the money was needed. The banks would go along, but not cheerfully. The prime rate on loans stood at just over 17 percent, and Danner knew the city would have to pay that and more.

Carl Gaines began to use the telephone in his austere office, then he thought better of it. Wiretaps weren't unheard of in politics. He felt vaguely guilty already for what he planned to do. But, like the mayor, he'd decided he had no choice.

He left his office, walked down the wide steps of City Hall, then crossed the sun-glazed street during a break in the traffic. On a corner a block away was a drugstore with a row of public phones. Gaines checked his pockets and found he had plenty of change. No need to risk impressing himself on the memory of one of the cashiers.

He waited for a woman wearing leg-hugging denim slacks, carrying an obviously expensive Gucci-monogrammed leather purse, to complete her rather animated phone conversation and leave. She was mumbling an Upper West Side address to herself as she walked away with rapid, mincing steps.

Gaines fed change to a telephone and direct-dialed a number he didn't have to look up in one of the mutilated directories. When the phone was answered he asked for the extension of Aaron Simpson, one of the governor's closest confidants.

He was told that Simpson was at his home, suffering the pain of an inflamed appendix. After thanking the crisp-voiced secretary and hanging up, Gaines fed the phone more silver and dialed Simpson's unlisted home number. Simpson owed him more than a few favors.

"How's the appendix?" Gaines asked, when Simpson had come to the phone.

"Like a lump of hot charcoal, Carl. But it'll quit hurting; it's done this before."

"Must be an inconvenience."

"And a damned painful one. What can I do for you, Carl?"

Gaines hesitated involuntarily for an instant, listening to the faint crackling on the line. "I need to talk to the governor, Aaron. Privately."

"It can be done. When?"

"As soon as possible."

"Should I tell him what about?"

"No. I'm sorry."

"I'll phone you back, Carl. Sometime this afternoon early. You going to be in your office?"

"I'll phone you, Aaron. How about one o'clock?"

"Good enough."

Gaines advised Simpson to set a date for an appendectomy and hung up.

68

11

From the fortieth-floor office window, the man with the full beard watched the building across the street. He sat straining forward in the dimness, eyes fitted into the rubber cups about the lenses of his high-powered Bushnell binoculars.

There was activity in 37-3. The bearded man made a note of the window location—thirty-seventh floor, third from the corner—on a small note pad by his right elbow. He raised the window slightly. Then he put down the binoculars and picked up a Minolta camera fitted with a bulky telephoto lens. He gazed through the viewfinder, moved the camera gently until he found window 37-3, and sat watching and waiting.

He felt the familiar warm tingling begin in his groin, radiate throughout his tense body. He was alone in the office. The regular employees had gone home hours ago. The bearded man was a part-time watchman, guarding the deserted offices of Compton Corporation, Insurance Brokers, until the full-time night watchman came on at ten. The bearded man's hours were from 6 to 10 P.M., five days a week. The pay wasn't top-scale, but it was something extra, and it gave him privacy and a place to watch from and satisfy what even he recognized as his curious compulsion.

A psychiatrist would classify him as a voyeur, he was sure. But didn't voyeurs usually have sexual hang-ups? The bearded man was proud that he had never had problems along that line. He simply enjoyed watching other people without their knowledge, really watching them, up close, while they did intimate things not necessarily connected with sex. Things like dining alone, reacting to reading or watching TV, combing their hair, speaking on the phone or examining themselves in a mirror. And sometimes they were stimulating to observe when they were not alone, when they argued, loved, hated, plotted, not knowing they were being observed as if by some celestial god as they moved along the surfaces of their lives.

Perhaps that was it, that secretly watching them made the bearded man feel somewhat like a god. Who wouldn't enjoy that? If they dared admit to themselves that they could feel that way.

He especially liked to observe the very rich, like the people across Fifty-seventh Street in the Beymer Building. Whoever that writer was who'd said that the rich were different knew what he was talking about. The rich had time to develop their vices and eccentricities; they didn't have to worry so much about mere survival. Or didn't think they did. Like the woman he'd seen in 29-12, when he'd spotted her that time from the fire stairs window. She was having sex with a man he was sure he'd seen before with another woman.

The bearded man often propped open the fortieth-floor fire door and traveled in a vertical line up and down his building so he could cover the Beymer Building completely, at least the side of it that faced his building. He had the freedom to do that; there was only one other person in the building during his working hours, another watchman on the sixth floor who seldom roamed.

And finally he had seen the man with the second woman again, in 34-7. This woman was a small, pretty brunette. The bearded man had managed to get some clear photographs of them through the telephoto lens. Once as they argued bitterly, once as the woman, near tears, stood staring out the window while the man stood behind her glaring at her. That was the bearded man's favorite of the photographs of those two. The woman hadn't known the man was watching her, and neither of them had known that their photograph was being taken. The special long-range photographic equipment the bearded man had bought was expensive, but it was shots like that one that made the expense worthwhile.

The other woman, the older one in 29-12, was also interesting. She would at times spend hours getting dressed in the mornings, trying on several obviously costly dresses, preening before a gold-framed mirror, painstakingly applying makeup. And often, after darkness, she seemed to enjoy walking nude about her apartment. Though when she did that she usually closed the sheer drapes and was little more than an occasionally glimpsed pacing form.

The bearded man caught another faint movement in 37-3. A woman he had seen only a few times before, a tall blonde with a long, straight nose and underslung chin, was standing near a sofa, just inside the window. The bearded man's camera clicked, the automatic winder whirred. Someone else, another woman, came into view. This woman was shorter, stockier, almost matronly, yet in an odd way prettier than the blond woman. They were speaking to each other. Arguing? The camera clicked and whirred repeatedly as the shorter woman stepped closer and inserted a hand beneath the blond woman's partially unbuttoned blouse.

The bearded man steadied his camera and chuckled softly, feeling the warmth spread along his stomach and legs. The rich! The rich had nothing better to do than this sort of thing. Or perhaps browse in the expensive antique shops and galleries that lined Fifty-seventh Street below.

The rich! Oh, they deserved to suffer along with everyone else in this world! They should be made to pay in currency more dear than dollars for their excesses. The high and vulgar deserved to be brought down to everyone else's level. Brought down to below that level.

12

Fourteen names.

That was what the computer in its electronic wisdom had kicked out for Canby to work with. And each name belonged to a demolition expert possessing enough skill to have destroyed the Morgell Trust Building.

Canby sat at his desk, watching the Lucite buttons on his telephone blink silently, then stop blinking, as the calls were handled outside his office. He sipped black coffee from a waxed cardboard cup on his desk corner. The coffee was getting cold fast, sitting in the direct breeze from the air conditioner. Canby reflected dismally that coffee didn't stay hot long in the flimsy cups issued by the balky, thieving vending machine in the downstairs cafeteria. From now on he'd send someone out for coffee.

He realized suddenly that he was dwelling on trivialities because he was getting nowhere struggling with the larger problem.

Most of the fourteen names had been routinely easy to

check. It hadn't taken long for nine of the names to be re-categorized as possible but unlikely. Three more names were eliminated because of death or long-term foreign residence. The problem was that since the explosives might have been planted years before being detonated, it was virtually impossible to eliminate a suspect entirely. No one could be expected to provide an alibi covering the past decade.

Canby sipped lukewarm coffee and stared down at the two remaining names on the list. Dimitri Kivas and Howard Lane. They were names that the computer categorized as "median gradient probability," whatever that meant in computerese.

Canby decided to check out one of the names personally, so he would at least get out of his office and experience some illusion of progress. He knew that he wasn't and never would be entirely a desk cop. But every year chained him more firmly to his desk. And even busy as he was, the sameness of his existence permitted sieges of loneliness.

In his youth, Canby had experienced the crushing isolation peculiar to poverty. He had been one of four brothers upon whom had fallen the responsibility of supporting their widowed mother from the time they were in their teens. That was why Canby had reluctantly and traumatically deserted his burgeoning art. It was Dexter, the youngest, who endured a succession of grimy, back-straining jobs to contribute most of the support. The oldest brother, Frank, lived now in California, retired from the Navy and growing oranges on a modest scale. The two middle brothers, Victor and Wendell, were dead, Victor of a heart attack a dozen years ago, Wendell from being struck by a streetcar thirty-two years ago. Wendell, Canby often reflected, would have been the most successful of the four.

During the years with Bernice, the loneliness that had seemed a natural part of Canby's life had withdrawn, waited dormant and dark to creep back after her death. He knew now that the isolation and pain of early poverty never really left the pockets of the soul. Bernice was gone, and despite bright moments with Molly Garrity, Canby was lonely again.

Norris buzzed and told Canby that Strother was on his way in.

Strother appeared to have more vitality than he had yesterday. His long face was still haggard, but his blue eyes gleamed with a faint touch of the fanatic's inspired strength.

"Anything, Captain?" he asked.

"We're still searching," Canby said.

"Any of the names pan out?"

"Not to speak of. The trouble is, we can't really *eliminate* most of them."

"Something like running on a treadmill," Strother said.

"Crawling on a treadmill," Canby corrected. He pushed his now icy coffee away in disdain. "There are two more names."

Strother's lean body seemed to come even more alive with a sudden charge of energy. "Why don't you give them to me to check out?"

Canby exhaled softly and wondered at the position in which he'd placed himself. What if one of these names did turn out to belong to the man they sought? What if that man panicked, shot Strother or took some other insane and violent course of action? Canby would be responsible, totally responsible.

There were mitigating circumstances: diminishing time, Strother's professional expertise. But if it came to an inquiry, these would seem like frail arguments in front of an investigatory board. Yet there were times when a man had to look beyond the job and self-interest and proceed on his instincts. And it was senseless to involve Strother in the investigation and not fully utilize him.

"I thought I'd check one of the names myself," Canby said. "You can have the other."

Strother walked to the desk and peered down at the list, adjusting his glasses. "Which name do I get?"

Canby glanced at the last known addresses after each name. Kivas's address wasn't immediately familiar; Lane's was in a rough section of town. "I'll take Lane," Canby said, "you get Kivas." He leaned back in his chair so he could stare up at Strother. "Just ask the basic questions we discussed. Don't

75

pretend to be a police officer, and for God's sake don't use your initiative. We're both on ice so thin it isn't cold."

Strother nodded and left, his lanky body moving with intrepid haste.

The telephone buzzed. Thorpe, wanting to know about any progress on the case. Canby told him there wasn't any, but that the investigation was still moving. Thorpe sounded disappointed when he said good-bye, which vaguely angered Canby. Thorpe knew how it was; the act wasn't necessary with Canby. Or had Thorpe forgotten how it was? That thought sobered Canby. In the near future, he might very much need Thorpe's support.

Canby picked up the list of names with Howard Lane's address on it and walked from his office, stopping at the desk on the way out to tell Norris he'd return soon.

Two uniformed patrolmen were wrestling a cursing, bloody-headed man in a tattered T-shirt toward the booking desk. "It ain't right!" the man screamed, thrashing violently but ineffectually. Canby barely glanced at the trio as he went out.

Howard Lane's address turned out to be that of the Grand Hall Hotel, a fifteen-story crumbling brick building surrounded by similar moribund buildings on St. Vincent Avenue in Brooklyn. Next to the lobby entrance was a combination pawnshop and adult bookstore.

Canby parked his unmarked gray car on the opposite side of the street and glanced around as he switched off the engine. There were a few people on the littered, sun-harshened sidewalks, walking either as if they had someplace to be in a hurry or as if they had no place to be at all. Some of the storefronts were boarded up, but most of them represented small, struggling businesses: a dry cleaner's, a used-camera shop, a liquor store. The neighborhood seemed to be a mixture of blacks, whites and Puerto Ricans. Canby radioed his location and got out of the car.

He walked past a large, yellowed poster of an unbelievably

contorted nude blonde and entered the Grand Hall Hotel's lobby. A long hall featuring ornate elevator doors and peeling paint ran to the main lobby with its threadbare red carpet and groupings of worn armchairs. Near the back exit, on the other side of the lobby, was a large artificial plant with long green stalks that seemed to bend toward the door and the sunlight as if in humorless jest. A thin balding man who was part of the dimness stood behind the desk, reading a newspaper. As Canby approached, the man glanced up and Canby was aware of being recognized as the Law.

Canby showed the desk man his badge, holding it out long enough for it to be meaninglessly studied. "You have a Howard Lane registered here?"

The man laughed. "Registered ain't exactly the word. Howie comes in now an' then for one of the cheap beds. When he's got the money and needs to be outa the weather."

"Is he here now?"

The balding man quickly checked his soiled registration book. He had a small round depression in his forehead near his temple, from a long-ago serious head injury. Possibly a bullet wound. And the lobe of his left ear was missing.

"Not here now," the man said, rotating the book to face Canby.

"Does he have a job?"

"Not Howie. He has a bottle, usually."

"Know where I might find him?"

"No, but I can phone you if he checks in here."

Canby was surprised by the offer. He thanked the desk clerk and started to leave.

"Wait a minute," the balding man said. "You maybe oughta try the Red Aid Blood Bank, two blocks over on Andrews."

Canby knew that many of the inner-city blood banks got most of their business from indigent drunks—mostly winos, since wine was cheap—who sold their blood for enough money to keep them in liquor and shelter. He had an insight into Howard Lane.

"Would you call Lane an alcoholic?" Canby asked.

The desk clerk shrugged. "He drinks cheap booze and a lot of it."

"Cheap wine?"

"Cheap anything. But wine mostly. You could call him a wino and not be far wrong. I heard him say once he needs wine to keep his red corpuscle count high so he can donate blood more often. You think there's anything to that?"

"Might be," Canby said, and walked from the diminished splendor of the Grand Hall Hotel.

He had to wait at the blood bank for less than an hour before Howard Lane showed up. An attendant had told Canby that the blood bank permitted many of the winos to stay in the waiting area, especially during inclement weather, and it had become something of a hangout for them lately because it was air-conditioned. Canby knew that the blood bank and the winos had a tacit agreement of mutual support.

When a skinny, shaggy-haired old man in a frayed shirt, secondhand pants and a worn pair of sneakers shambled in through the door, the attendant Canby had talked to nodded. Canby rose from the uncomfortable wooden folding chair on which he sat and walked toward Howard Lane along one of the aisles formed by the rows of chairs.

In a strange way Lane seemed to become younger as Canby approached. His skin was unshaven but firm, and many of the lines in his face were accentuated by a film of dirt. His teeth were bad, and his eyes were aged, but other than that it was as if the head of a man in his mid-forties had been placed on a seventy-year-old decrepit body.

Lane's lips drew back and the faded eyes grew large with alarm as Canby loomed near.

"Howard Lane?"

Lane recognized the voice of officialdom and swallowed, hesitantly nodding.

Canby showed his identification. "I need to talk to you for a minute, Mr. Lane."

Lane nodded again, swallowed again, and Canby led him

78

toward a private corner. Canby noticed the reek of stale whiskey and the perspiration stench of long-unwashed clothes. And he could smell Lane's fear.

When they'd sat down, Canby saw that Lane's hands were trembling in a riot of movement impossible to control.

"You from the welfare people?" Lane asked.

Canby shook his head no. "How long has it been since you've worked?" he asked, realizing that he sounded like a welfare caseworker.

"Been eight . . . nine years." An unsteady forearm dragged a grimy shirt-sleeve across dry lips.

"Where was your last job?"

Lane surprised Canby. "Mexico City. I used to be a demolition man, one of the best." He didn't seem at all unhappy to be using the past tense. "Mexican government hired me to help 'em demolish some old buildings to make way for a development project. I was there four years an' came down sick. I ain't been all the way right since."

"Sick how?"

"Hell, I don't remember the medical name. Starts with a *B*. It was somethin' that ruined me with fever, somethin' I caught from bad well water."

"You start to drink liquor heavily in Mexico, Howard?"

"Before. Long time before. But in Mexico was where I found myself all of a sudden inside the bottle. I figured booze was better than the drugs that was goin' around there at the time. But I drank myself outa my job an' a good woman besides."

"Maybe you'd be dead now if you'd opted for drugs."

"Maybe I am dead."

Canby studied Lane carefully. If the emaciated man was putting on an act, it was a hell of a good act. His entire body seemed poised, tingling with sensitive nerve endings and apprehension.

"Mister," Lane said softly, "I got myself buried alive in Mexico. I mean really, for over twenty-four hours. A building come down all around me because some damned Mex

79

laborer tripped the explosives. I could breathe but barely, an' when they dug me free it turned out both my legs was broken an' more ribs than they could count. Then I got the sickness, an' it was six months later I come home." Lane's lips were quivering now, and his tongue darted along the jumble of his rotted teeth.

Canby extended his lower lip and nodded. "Thanks for talking to me, Mr. Lane." He shook hands warmly with Lane and stood up.

As he turned to leave, Canby suddenly whirled and slapped one of the folding chairs to the cement floor so sharply that it made a sound like a clattering hammer blow. Lane let out a whining whistle and cowered back in the corner, whimpering and refusing to look at Canby. He was trembling violently, his hands folded into each other as if broken. His suffering was genuine.

The attendant was staring at Canby with mouth slack and eyes blank.

Depressed about subjecting Lane to such a test, Canby hesitated, then walked quickly from the blood bank. The sun struck him with an almost palpable force, slowing his stride.

He needed a drink.

13

Dimitri Kivas's address was that of an old but well-maintained brick flat in a neighborhood that had reached a very advanced age gracefully. Strother stepped into the stifling tiny vestibule, smelled something pungent and no doubt delicious cooking, and checked the names above the tarnished brass mailboxes. There was no Kivas in 4C, where the police department list had Kivas living, or in any of the other flats.

The slot above 4C's mailbox read "F. Compross." Strother pressed the door buzzer and started up the rubber-treaded wood stairs.

When he reached the second floor, the door to 4C was wide open and a stout woman in a flower-print dress was standing staring at him. She had astoundingly gelatinous upper arms and a faint dark mustache.

"Miss Compross?" Strother asked, taking the final steep step.

"Mrs."

"My name is Strother. I'm looking for a Mr. Dimitri Kivas. He used to live here."

"Not anymore. I live here three years."

"Alone?"

"Why?" Dark eyes set deep in fleshy cheeks narrowed.

Strother was momentarily thrown. "I, uh . . . Do you know who lived here before you moved in?" Safer ground, but not fertile.

"Don't know or care." Mrs. Compross shook her head firmly. "I rent," she added, as if to explain.

Strother tried his smile. "I'm not attempting to pry, Mrs. Compross, believe me. But it's important that I locate Mr. Kivas." He considered telling her that a great deal of money was involved, then he remembered that in an indirect way he represented the police department.

"My lamb stew."

"What?"

"It's burning," Mrs. Compross said, and shut the door.

Strother stood alone, burning along with the lamb stew. Then he turned and tromped angrily down the stairs, pausing at the landing to gaze out a window at the time-beaten but clean neighborhood. It might never become a genuine slum, might continue this way for years, kept alive by the old values of its longtime hardcore residents.

When Strother reached the first floor, he saw that one of the doors was partly open. A small, gray-haired woman with a round, dried-apple face stared out at him, smiling toothlessly.

"I heard," she said, pointing upward with a gnarled finger. "I'm the super here. I knew Mr. Kivas." From behind her stunted figure, the unmistakable odor of cat urine wafted from her flat. "You step in?"

Strother tried to place her accent, which was much like Mrs. Compross's. Possibly Greek. The name "Kivas" sounded Greek. Maybe this was one of the old areas of the city populated by Greeks or whatever ethnic group to which the building's super and Mrs. Compross belonged.

The old woman stepped back, and Strother entered the flat. The stench of cat urine was suddenly overpowering. He

82

got an impression of high, overstuffed furniture, antimacassars and countless knickknacks in faded light filtered through lace blinds. An ominously large gray cat with white forepaws lay curled on the rounded arm of a chair.

"Better that Mrs. Compross doesn't know who lived in the flat before her," the old woman said conspiratorially.

"Why?"

"I knew Mr. Kivas and his wife," she said, ignoring Strother's question. "They live here several years. We were of the same church, of the old Herras religion."

"Where did he move to, do you know?"

"Ah, dead."

"What?"

The woman touched an arthritically twisted hand to the side of her neck, an oddly mournful gesture. "Dead. Mr. Kivas died upstairs three years ago. That's why I never tell Mrs. Compross. Tenants, you never know . . ."

"How did Mr. Kivas die?" Strother didn't know why he asked the question. It simply seemed the path their conversation should take.

"Cancer," the woman said in her cracking voice. "We prayed for him, but he died. His time." She reached out a hand and lightly brushed Strother's elbow, as if it were a touchstone of youth.

Strother felt that it would be his time if he couldn't escape from the odorous flat. There was nothing more to talk about. He'd found out what he needed to know. He thanked the old woman and backed out the door, into the hall.

She smiled at him with the remnants of some lost maternal instinct as he descended the final short flight of stairs to the vestibule and pushed open the door to the street.

Standing outside in the sunshine, he realized he hadn't asked the woman's name. That wasn't reason enough for him to go back in. Strother walked to his car, looking about at the lettering on some of the neighborhood shops. Below the English, here and there was printing in what might have been Hebrew or Greek. He couldn't tell which, if either.

His car was parked in front of a small shoe-repair shop. Halfway down the block, three swarthy, dark-haired youths in tank-top shirts were lounging, leaning in exaggerated fashion against a brick wall as if casually keeping it from falling. Strother felt his heart accelerate, and he inwardly primed himself for trouble. But the two boys who looked his way smiled amiably at him, turned and continued talking.

As he started his car, Strother hoped Canby had found some luck with Howard Lane.

14

Canby met Molly that evening at Durell's Restaurant on East Sixtieth Street. Durell's was a small restaurant, built on two levels, the lower of which was lined with high-backed private booths. Adjoining the upper level was a tiny lounge, where customers could drink while waiting for tables on busier nights. Durell's was paneled in natural walnut, pleasantly lighted by antique ceiling fixtures, and counted among its customers many of the city's sports and entertainment figures. The food was good, the music that filtered in from the lounge soft, and the waiters were attentive but otherwise invisible.

When Canby arrived, Molly was waiting for him in the restaurant's small foyer. Maury the maître d' led them to the corner booth they usually occupied when they dined at Durell's. Around them the walls were decorated with antique photographs, some of them tintypes, in ornate frames. Faces of the long dead, who never dreamed when the camera clicked and the flash powder exploded that their likenesses would far in the future adorn the walls of Durell's Restaurant and be contemplated by strangers.

Canby was brought his customary before-dinner manhattan, Molly her daiquiri. Molly was wearing a dark green blouse that even in the dimness brought out the fiery redness of her hair. A gold earring on her left earlobe caught the light from the lounge and winked into Canby's mind a vision of the desk clerk at the Grand Hall Hotel. And of Howard Lane.

For a while it had bothered Canby that Lane's story was so pat. But it had all checked out. Lane had been in Mexico until eight years ago, and from there had gone almost directly into a hospital in Lexington, Kentucky, to shake his alcoholism. The hospital hadn't helped. His health and nerves shot, Lane had been a penniless, hopeless alcoholic since his return from Mexico, a demolition expert working slow but complete destruction on himself.

"I take it things aren't going well," Molly said, laying the swizzle stick from her drink on the white napkin beneath the glass. She always laid her swizzle stick crossways, parallel to the napkin edge, as if it were a tiny barrier Canby must not yet cross.

"It seems as if things are going nowhere," he said.

Molly took a sip of her daiquiri, looking at him over the glass rim. "What about Militants for the Millions?" she asked, returning glass to napkin.

"I checked them out. They were a mid-sixties protest group that straggled into the seventies, then all but disbanded. The so-called regional director is a grown-up student radical named Dennis Benson who lives in a run-down house over on Favor Street in the Bronx."

"Has someone talked to Benson?"

"Sure. He says he didn't send the letter claiming responsibility for Morgell Trust. We're keeping close tabs on him, but there are no grounds right now to bring him in or suspect that he or his disbanded organization had anything to do

86

with the demolition. Even when they were young and in their heyday, they never did anything violent."

"People and organizations change."

"But there is no more organization to speak of. Benson claims only ten members now, and he hasn't seen most of them in over a year, when they had a Fourth of July picnic."

"So who do you think sent the letter?"

Canby shrugged, rotated the damp bottom of his glass on the tablecloth. "Who sends letters like that? Could be some crackpot with a grudge against Militants for the Millions, or maybe against Benson personally. Maybe it was an ex-member who got drunk and yearned for the activist days of his youth. There's no reason to take that letter any more seriously than most of the other fringe-sanity mail we've received since the Morgell Trust Building came down."

"I wouldn't be so sure," Molly said. "I have a feeling about that one . . ."

The waiter came and they ordered, Canby a sirloin, Molly her usual filet mignon. Canby asked for another drink.

"My instincts tell me it's a nothing," Canby said. But he'd learned to have respect for Molly's intuition, for almost anyone's intuition. Sometimes he thought that when you boiled away the procedure, intuition was all there was of police work.

Their salads arrived, then their steaks, and they ate silently. There was a current of uneasiness between them. The girl at the piano bar in the lounge was singing a romantic lament familiar to Canby, but he couldn't quite make out the words or recall the name of the song. He only knew that it wasn't one of his favorites.

"Who is this Strother who's been helping you?" Molly asked, buttering a roll.

"He was the Morgell Trust Building's architect. He got a rough deal because of what happened, and he came to me with an offer to help."

"Do you think it's wise to take him up on that offer?"

"No, but his personal involvement and zeal could break the case."

"Or break you."

Canby was becoming vaguely annoyed by her persistent fencing. He cut a piece from his rare steak and watched the pinkish blood run to the center of his plate. "I thought hard about it before letting Strother get involved. I know I might be broken for it, but I felt I had to take the chance."

"As a human being, not a cop."

"I try not to differentiate between the two."

"You know what I mean, Dex. I don't want you hurt."

Canby knew how she'd intended the remark. He was being too rough on her.

"Dex, there's another reason I feel so strongly that Militants for the Millions might be involved." She was staring down at her baked potato as she spoke, as if it might be the most intelligent thing on her plate and would understand. "I was what you might call a sixties radical. I'd been out of college awhile, without a degree, but I saw what the ultra-rich establishment was doing to us then, and I became politically involved."

"Who wasn't at that time?"

"I mean I was an activist, in on demonstrations."

"Violent demonstrations?"

"I didn't indulge in any violence myself, and I didn't belong to any violent organizations. But sometimes the demonstrations became violent. It was inevitable. What I'm trying to say is, I know better than you know how these people think. I was one of them, and I can tell you there's a certain type that won't quit no matter what the political climate. They thrive on ferment; they need it."

She was right, Canby knew. He'd been on the other side of the fence in the sixties, a "pig" who'd seen what some of the political demonstrations could turn into. He could still remember the distorted, fervent faces of some of the activists for whom the movement was only a stage on which they could play out the desperate dreams of their own frustra-

88

tions and fears. For some, those emotions must still be very real.

"I'll have Benson questioned again," he told Molly.

She seemed relieved. "I'd feel better, Dex. It might mean so much, so many lives . . ."

Her flowing hair picked up all the light in the room and held it, and her green eyes seemed to draw him to cool depths. Sensitive to light and shadow, he wished that when he was younger he could have painted her.

But now he was almost fifty, and beyond all that.

"Do you want dessert?" he asked.

"Just coffee," she said. "Then I'd like to go home. With you."

Maybe fifty was only the late summer of life.

15

Helice Gorham beat a bare heel against Vish's buttocks in a sudden wild tattoo. They were in Helice's apartment on the twenty-ninth floor of the Beymer Building, in Helice's queen-sized bed. Vish had reached sexual climax seconds before. He could never tell if Helice was actually achieving orgasm or faking. But then he didn't care.

Her sigh changed to a lazy musical moan, and he raised his upper body to support himself with his arms, his fists sunk deep into the soft mattress. Helice was staring languidly up at him from the tangled design of her dark hair. Vish moved clumsily away from her, to the other side of the bed, kissing her shoulder to dispel the sense of desolation that suddenly bound them.

He lay silently and looked about at the quietly and tastefully decorated bedroom. The walls were pale blue, the furniture white French provincial and expensive. Beyond cream-colored sheer drapes, peaks of buildings loomed like dark watchful figures. Always in Helice's bedroom was the faint lilac scent of the perfume she wore.

Vish actually lived five floors above, in a similar but not so tastefully decorated apartment, with his wife Wilma. He had in the past few years achieved a surprising measure of fame and wealth as a drama critic whose column was syndicated to more than a hundred newspapers as well as a national magazine. That was why he could now afford to live in the Beymer Building, which was a forty-two-story bastion of wealth, featuring an electronic security system, a doorman at the residents' entrance, and a somehow haughty architectural design of pale cast concrete, stainless steel and glass.

The lower four floors of the Beymer Building, served by a separate elevator system, consisted of offices, and in the lobby were a great many potted plants, an expensive beauty salon, and a small coffee shop that specialized in good food at surprisingly reasonable prices.

Vish, a chunky, slope-shouldered man with an inordinate amount of hair over his pale body, rose from the bed and walked nude into the small bathroom adjoining Helice's bedroom. His dark hairline was receded to form a sharp widow's peak, and he wore a carefully trimmed goatee, lending his otherwise blunted features a pugnacious, eager look. Water ran in the bathroom, and he returned a moment later and stepped into his undershorts and pants.

Helice was still lying on her back with her eyes lightly closed. As he sat on her vanity stool to put on his shoes and socks, Vish studied her. She was still a beautifully proportioned woman though approaching her fiftieth year. The tanned flesh of her face was darker than the rest of her body, with fine crinkles about her gray eyes and a clue to her age at her throat. She had the sort of symmetrical, bold facial bone structure that resisted the toll of accumulated years, and from a distance Helice might indeed pass for thirty-five. She was a fashion buyer for a chain of exclusive women's shops, and she could use clothes and makeup skillfully to create the illusion of youth.

Vish was thirty-five though he appeared forty, and at times he experienced the vague notion that while he was growing

91

ever older Helice was becoming ever younger, and at some point they physiologically would be exactly the same age.

"Would you like a drink?" he asked her.

"Thanks, no," she said, still with her eyes closed.

Vish stood up, catching a glimpse of his shirtless torso in the vanity mirror. The mirror's ornate softly curved edging seemed a suitable frame for what he saw. Someday he would have to do something about the paunch. He put on his white dress shirt, then a dark maroon tie. Wilma thought he was attending a performance of a play that actually he'd seen last week, and he was due back home soon. It was raining outside; he might sprinkle a bit of water from the washbasin faucet onto the shoulders of his coat for a touch of authenticity. He was amused by the thought, but fine detail really wasn't necessary to fool Wilma.

Behind Vish, Helice had risen and put on a royal-blue silk robe. She gave her hair a practiced shake and pulled the robe's long sash belt tight about her thickening waist.

"I wonder," she said.

"Wonder aloud," Vish suggested. Where Helice was standing, the early evening light softened by the sheer curtains flattered her. He was sure the effect was calculated.

"You're a relatively young man, Harold. And Wilma is, though I hate to admit it, a damned attractive woman even younger than you. Why is it you prefer my company?"

"Seeking compliments?"

"No, I don't want bullshit." She smiled. "At least not right now. I just can't help being a little curious."

"You're a woman of experience"—Vish adjusted his tie knot—"as well as beauty and style."

"I'm still curious, Harold. Is something . . . wrong with Wilma?"

Vish shrugged into his tailor-cut gray sport jacket. "She watches Lawrence Welk reruns," he said.

Helice laughed. "Hardly a grievous sin."

"Not a sin, no . . . This, adultery, is more of a sin. Yet somehow I find it more forgivable."

"Someday, Harold, you're going to have to grow up and stop being a romantic snob."

"Not today." He walked into the living room and put on his raincoat.

Helice followed him. "You know what I think you like most about me?" she asked. When Vish didn't answer, she said, "When the time comes, you know I can let go." She said this without rancor, more with philosophical objectivity. "No soap opera complications."

"Has the time come?" Vish asked.

She kissed him adroitly, with lips and tongue, holding his head delicately between her long-nailed, manicured hands. "Not quite yet," she said, stepping away from him.

She had technique and knew tricks, all right, Vish reflected appreciatively. Wilma knew no tricks.

Vish smiled at Helice as he left the apartment. He knew she needed his adoration, even if she suspected it wasn't totally sincere. Her need was something of life's prime for her to hang on to; it helped to slow her slide.

In 29D, the apartment next door to Helice's, James Boston straightened up from where he was sitting with his ear pressed near the air-conditioning vent. His apartment and Helice Gorham's shared the ductwork in the separating wall, and Boston was listening as he often did to Helice's amorous activities in the bedroom less than a foot away. He sat back in the low, comfortable armchair he kept in his bedroom expressly for listening purposes and absently reached down and petted Arlo, his gray miniature schnauzer. Arlo wagged his stubby tail, sneezed and sat down.

James Boston was a retired importer. He was still an advisory-board member of Boston-Farr, the company he'd helped found. But for the first time in his sixty-two years there actually was nothing of importance to demand his attention. A slim, impeccably dressed man with thinning hair and a shopworn jaunty manner, he wore a graying pencil-thin mustache that he fancied made him resemble a leading

93

man of the Ronald Colman era. Other than his daily trips to his brokerage house to sit and study the stock market quotations, his principal activity was prying into his neighbors' affairs.

Boston disliked Helice Gorham. She'd been unfriendly toward him since the time six months ago when he complained about certain late-night noises coming from her apartment. Well, he no longer complained. Not since discovering that listening at his bedroom vent was almost like being in the same room with Helice Gorham.

Wilma Vish, on the other hand, Boston liked. She was a smallish brunette with wistful dark eyes, never without an answering hello or a word of good cheer. A graceful, considerate woman still in her early thirties, she was, in Boston's estimation, ever so much more attractive than Helice Gorham.

Boston had often thought about informing Wilma Vish of her husband's trysts with Helice Gorham. It would be simple, a brief anonymous phone call. And the delayed reaction in the Gorham apartment would be interesting. Boston had done such things before; it was not so much meddling as setting things right. Wilma Vish certainly deserved better than what was going on.

And Harold Vish certainly didn't . . . well, he certainly didn't deserve *two* women, even if one of them was Helice Gorham. He was in many ways a cruel and callous man. Boston remembered Vish's reaction down in the coffee shop to the news of that Morgell Trust Building falling with all those people inside. "God's telling us we should have built a parking lot there," Vish had said, and even Myra behind the counter hadn't laughed. What if the Beymer Building should have been a parking lot?

Several times Boston's elegant hand had gone to his telephone to dial Wilma Vish's number. But always the hand had stopped.

There was something about Harold Vish that frightened Boston.

Boston glanced at his watch. Seven o'clock. Not yet time to take Arlo for his walk. Boston could faintly hear Helice Gorham puttering around in her bedroom, probably cleaning up the mess, getting dressed.

After a few minutes the noises ceased, and Boston heard a remote hissing sound. Helice Gorham was showering.

His expression intent, Boston sat thinking about that until the hissing stopped. Then he decided to go down to the lobby for a cup of coffee and a chat with Myra, the waitress. Myra was always good for a joke or a laugh.

Boston left Arlo with a meat-flavored dog treat and went downstairs.

Across the street, the man with the full beard sat holding his binoculars in his lap. There had been no opportunity for photographs, but there was little doubt in the bearded man's mind as to what had gone on behind the sheer drapes of window 29-12 on the other side of Fifty-seventh Street. He had seen the man and woman with each other before, when the drapes had not been closed to reduce his vision to wavering, indistinct human forms. Forms coming together, separating, joining again and again.

Now the man had left. What would the woman do? Whatever she did, the bearded man was sure it wouldn't be cheap. A stroll in her hundred-dollar Gucci shoes to shop at Yves St. Tropez or Bergdorf Goodman? Then along Fifth Avenue to Tiffany's to examine a few gaudy baubles? To West Forty-fourth to meet friends for drinks at the sedate, richly paneled Algonquin? Lunch tomorrow in the Russian Tea Room?

The bearded man spat on the floor. He knew the haunts of the rich, and despised even the feel of those names in his mouth. The lives of the wealthy were an affront to the dignity of others, of the breathing corpses in the Bowery, the blind men begging on the sidewalks, the thousands of waiters, messengers, struggling accountants and street-corner peddlers looking only as far ahead as they dared. An affront to the dignity of people like himself.

95

Only death evened the situation. Plain pine boxes and satin-lined gilded coffins were all the same to their occupants. From the time of the pharaohs and their pyramids, the splendors of the grave had been wasted on the dead.

For the bearded man, that was an oddly comforting thought. He picked up his binoculars once more and fitted them to his eyes.

16

The phone beside Canby's bed jangled loudly at three the next morning. He grasped the shrill sound like an unexpected lifeline and pulled himself up from a dream of the thunder of crashing, ancient walls, wailing trumpet blasts and dead faces, recognizable and unrecognizable. Relief swept through him as his hand closed on the receiver, a more solid reality than he'd been experiencing. In the darkness, he lifted the receiver and drew it to his ear. The plastic earpiece felt cool; he was perspiring.

"Hello . . ." His voice was still detached by sleep.

There was a click, then a prolonged buzz as the connection was broken.

Canby glanced at the right-angled luminous hands of his clock-radio. A sick joke, he told himself, replacing the receiver. But he knew he couldn't get back to sleep right away. Just then, after a night of dark dreams, he too much preferred wakefulness.

He switched on the bedside reading lamp and sat up, trying to think of who might have his private number and would stoop to such a prank. Then he realized the call might just as easily have been made by kids who had strung together the required number of digits at random. He stood and walked into the kitchen, opened the refrigerator and used its feeble light to see to get a glass from the cupboard and pour himself some milk.

Canby was raising the glass to his lips when the explosion outside made his hand jump and milk slop over the glass's rim and onto the tiled floor. A fork slid from the counter and dropped into the sink with a reverberating clatter.

The sound of the explosion had come from the west side of the building, from the apartment complex's parking lot. Canby quickly returned to the bedroom, switching on lights as he went, and put on a pair of leather slippers and a bathrobe. Then he went to the living room window and looked down into the parking lot and saw his car burning.

The only way he knew it was his car was that it was in his private parking slot. The roof was peeled halfway off like the lid of a sardine can, and the trunk and hood were raised by the force of the blast. The interior was still burning, and several spectators attracted by the noise had the good sense to stay well back in case of a secondary gasoline explosion. Canby left his apartment and took the elevator down.

When he reached the parking lot he was surprised at how hot the weather was at such an early hour. A hundred feet to his right, near the building's main entrance, sat the blazing car. The stench of scorched metal and smoldering rubber tainted the humid night, and black smoke rose in twisting vapors to merge with the dark sky and drift shadowlike across the stars. In the distance, sirens wailed like frenzied, mournful coyotes.

The Fire Department appeared first, set up rudimentary crowd control and extinguished the flames with dry chemicals. Before the fire was out, two police cruisers from the seventeenth arrived simultaneously, parking near the driveway with their dome lights flashing. Canby recognized all four men in the cars. One of them was a young patrolman named Higby whose wife had recently been killed in an automobile accident.

Higby looked at Canby, not recognizing him wearing robe and slippers, then did a slow double take.

"Captain . . ." he said uncertainly.

"I don't go out on calls dressed like this," Canby said to put him at ease. "I live here."

Higby grinned. He was a tall, rangy man with quizzical eyes that reflected a generous measure of composure. "Do you know whose car it is, sir?"

"Mine."

Higby wasn't visibly surprised by the information. He rested the palm of his hand on his leather holster flap and nodded, glancing at the blackened wreckage of the unmarked police car.

"Tell the other cruiser to call back into service," Canby said. "You and your partner stay here and make sure nobody touches what's left of the car until the bomb squad arrives."

"Yes, sir." Higby appeared to want to say more, but he turned briskly and walked away to execute Canby's orders. In the wavering red glare of the rotating dome lights, multiple shadows writhed at the heels of his striding figure.

Canby went back up to his apartment and phoned the seventeenth, told Kelleher, the on-duty desk man, what had happened and had him dispatch the bomb squad to the scene.

Then he sat at the kitchen table, waiting, sipping his glass of tepid milk. He wished, now that it was impossible, that he could go back to bed.

Canby had managed only a few hours' sleep after the bomb squad left. Then he had to rise and leave for his office.

Once he'd taken a cold shower and come fully awake, he didn't mind staying up and was eager to get to the precinct house. He wanted to talk to Felstein about what, if anything, the bomb squad had ascertained.

Felstein was waiting for Canby at the seventeenth, leaning casually on the booking desk and chatting with Norris. There were a few patrolmen at the metal office desks, laboring over reports, and from Mathews' office came the sound of a mild argument. Canby didn't want to know what the argument was about. It was Mathews' problem.

"You want coffee this morning, Captain?" Norris asked.

"Not if it's that cow piss from the machine downstairs," Canby said. He had no reason to be in a good mood; someone had only hours ago blown up his car. He motioned with his head and walked into his office. Felstein followed.

The office was cool. At least Norris had remembered to turn on the air conditioner. Canby felt some slight remorse at having wisecracked Norris. He walked to the air conditioner and slapped it to stop its squealing, then sat down behind his desk.

Felstein, dressed in a neat brown summer-weight suit and pale yellow shirt and tie, sat down calmly in one of the chairs on the other side of the desk and waited in his unfathomable manner. He looked cool enough to frost glass.

"What did you find out from the wreckage?" Canby asked. He watched Felstein leisurely light a cigarette.

"Not who did it," Felstein said, capping his gold lighter and placing it back in his pocket. "Or why. But we did discover a few things about how." He exhaled a cloud of white smoke and the breeze from the air conditioner found it and shredded it. "The explosive agent was what's sometimes known as a plastique. It's a highly malleable explosive that can be worked like putty and placed in the damnedest unsuspected spots. In this case, it was placed beneath the dashboard of your car, and it appears that it was wired to explode when you turned your ignition key."

"Then why didn't it?"

Felstein held his cigarette at an angle and looked at it as if the answer might be written on its paper. "That we can't tell for sure. Too much evidence was destroyed by the blast and ensuing fire, not to mention the effects of the firefighting equipment. It could be that a mistake was made when the bomb was wired—some insulation heated up and shorted out the wiring or completed a circuit."

"This might sound silly, but would the explosion have proved fatal if I'd been behind the wheel?" Felstein's expert opinion would help to make it, officially, attempted murder.

Felstein's answer was considered, but it was firmly spoken. "They'd never have found all of you, Captain."

"How do you think the phone call I received a few minutes before the explosion ties in?"

"A lot of things are possible." Felstein leaned forward and used a manicured finger to flick cigarette ash into the brass ashtray on the desk. "Maybe the phone call was meant to get you to go out and start your car, and the caller muffed his job and didn't say what he was supposed to."

"Could the explosion have been set off by a timer? Maybe it had nothing to do with the ignition at all."

Felstein shook his head no. "Not unless a timer was used for a backup detonator. We found where one of the ignition wires had been spliced. My guess, Captain, is that the phone call was coincidental, some drunk dialing a wrong number and realizing it, then hanging up. Or maybe somebody dialed wrong and thought you were someone's husband and didn't want to talk. Coincidence is the only way I can see the call; you'd have received it whether or not your car was wired to blow."

Canby sat staring at his unopened mail. What Felstein had said was the most likely explanation, and the dapper lieutenant had an uncanny feel for the psychology of those who planted explosives for whatever tormented and twisted reasons. Sometimes Felstein made Canby uneasy. Canby began to wonder if his phone had actually rung, or if he'd imagined it as an escape from his dreams.

"Aren't plastic bombs the sort used most often by political terrorists?" he asked.

Felstein drew on his cigarette and nodded. "It's a stable substance and suited for their purpose. There's practically no danger of it exploding until it's wired." He paused, letting smoke filter in languid tendrils from his nostrils.

"Something else, Captain," he said calmly. "We got a call at eight this morning. A maintenance crew in the Chadner Arms over on Fifth Avenue was doing some repair work on leaky plumbing. When they cut through some foundation cement with an air hammer they discovered an oilskin packet that contained blasting powder. They notified us and we looked further at the structure's load-bearing points, and discovered enough explosives to bring down the building. There was a detonating device that could be activated by a code of high-frequency, short-range electronic signals."

Canby felt a cool excitement gain strength and course through him. Was it possible that a piece of luck, a chance discovery, would break the case? "Has the lab figured out the code?"

"They're working on it. But that really wouldn't help us much. Not unless we knew the specific target building and could be there with the right equipment to jam the bomber's transmission."

"What about fingerprints?"

"None. They were only glove smears, and smudges where prints had been wiped off clean."

Canby's excitement was slowly changing to anger. "So there's not even a slim hope that it's a wild bluff—"

"No, sir. And when these explosives were found, I remembered something and did some checking. Five years ago, similar explosives were discovered in a building on Nineteenth Street. They were removed and the affair was kept quiet. There might be dozens—or more—buildings out there rigged to be brought down."

"Isn't there any way to locate them? Suppose we make up a list of buildings constructed or remodeled during the past twelve years? Could you use some sort of equipment to check them for explosive charges?"

"There wouldn't be time, Captain. And we can't go rushing in with sledge hammers or even sophisticated electronic equipment, because we can't be sure all the explosive charges are wired to the type of detonator we found in the Chadner Arms. Remember, a plastique was used in your car."

"Maybe our bomber has become more sophisticated."

"Plastiques have been used for more than a decade. So it's not a matter of advancing technology. That type of explosive gained notoriety in France in the early sixties."

Canby stood up, feeling a sudden dizziness from lack of sleep and from the outside relentless heat that couldn't be kept entirely at bay. "Keep me informed," he said to Felstein, "on everything."

Felstein nodded as he stood. Before going out the door, he said, "The lab's still working on your car, Captain, but I doubt they can come up with anything more."

It occurred for the first time to Canby that Felstein was one of those people who habitually leave a conversation on a note of pessimism. Or realism.

Canby sat back down and thought about plastic bombs and political terrorists of the sixties and of the oddly surrealistic view from his third-floor apartment window of his destroyed, burning car. He felt depressingly alone within himself. Everyone was essentially alone, he decided. Some of us, if we're decent, give aid and comfort. Others of us seize what we can to dampen our desperation. And that made work for Canby.

He shook himself out of that mental rut. Dangerous thoughts for a cop.

He got Mathews on the phone and instructed him to have Dennis Benson of Militants for the Millions brought in for questioning.

17

James Boston sat at the counter in the Beymer Coffee Shop in the lobby of the Beymer Building. Usually he had his breakfast at one of the tables, but lately he'd fallen into the habit of chatting with Myra the counter girl as he ate. Myra was observant if not very intelligent, and what knowledge she possessed could easily be extracted in slyly oblique ways by Boston. Between bites of bacon-and-cheese omelet, he learned a great deal about his neighbors.

The coffee shop was small, with groupings of tiny round tables and with a marble-veined Formica countertop marked with a design that matched exactly that of the tile floor. That duplication of design often intrigued Boston and in small ways affected his appetite. Sometimes as he was lifting his fork or spoon he almost expected to see the parading cuffs and shoes of passersby. For his own morbid amusement, he carried the inane vision further and imagined a shiny brown wing-tip shoe carelessly kicking aside his plate and silverware. He knew that these idle reflections were a result of suddenly having too much time on his hands.

Myra delivered a cup of coffee and a breakfast roll to one of the tables, then returned to her station behind the counter. She was a tall, plain-featured woman who at work wore a perfect expression of servitude and kept her dark but gray-flecked hair in a practical neat bun at the nape of her neck. Her left arm was badly scarred as if it had been burned, and on the bridge of her nose was an unattractive mole that a doctor might easily remove. Myra could have been thirty or fifty or any age so bracketed. Boston occasionally wondered about her personal life.

She refilled his white ceramic coffee mug and leaned relaxed with her elbow on the counter.

"Do you know Mrs. Vish?" Boston asked, taking a small bite of omelet.

"Never talked to her," Myra said, "but I know her by sight. Pretty woman. She comes in now an' then for lunch. Usually a turkey-and-bacon club and a Coke."

"She's the wife of Harold Vish, the drama critic."

"Him we both know," Myra said, raising a dark eyebrow, as if she were an actress Vish had slighted in a review.

Boston sipped his coffee and gave a high, snickering laugh. "I could tell you some things about that one. But then I suppose you know more than I do. You're in a position where you can't help but hear things."

"People talk around you if you're a waitress," Myra agreed. "They get used to you and don't know you're there. Or maybe they don't care."

"Well, if people don't want things repeated they shouldn't talk about them in front of other people."

"Especially if they don't leave a tip."

"The ones with a lot of money," Boston said, "they're usually the cheapest. You can believe that Vish is more than just well off."

"Do you know Mrs. Gorham?" Myra asked.

"I've met her," Boston said noncommittally. Apparently Myra didn't know he and Helice Gorham were next-door neighbors. "The lady on the twenty-ninth floor."

"That's her. A habitual ham on rye. Anyway, I saw her in here one time with Vish. They acted like they came in and met casually, but I could tell they had something to talk about."

"You don't think there's anything—"

"Goin' on between them? Naw, a guy like Vish would give a lady like Mrs. Gorham the creeps. He does me. I don't know what they were talking about."

"Still," Boston said, "I've heard rumors about Mrs. Gorham."

"You mean about why Mr. and Mrs. Caldwell moved?"

Boston nodded, though he'd never heard of the Caldwells.

"That was before you moved in," Myra said. "I hear there was quite a row over that affair, but Mr. Caldwell denied everything. That didn't keep Mrs. Caldwell from going after him with a knife. At least that's what I heard from Ginny the maid. Finally Mr. Caldwell agreed they'd move, I think to another city."

"Where was Helice Gorham when all this was going on?"

Myra glanced about and laughed softly, so that only Boston could hear. "Seems she had to visit a sick brother in Chicago."

"So you think she was really involved with Caldwell."

"I know it. Ginny found some of Mrs. Gorham's things once in the Caldwell apartment. That's what started the row."

"What sort of things?" Boston asked. "They might have gotten there in a perfectly innocent fashion."

"I don't know exactly, but they were what you might call intimate items."

Two men Boston knew only as Ray and Gary, uniformed deliverymen of some sort who daily had breakfast in the coffee shop, slid onto stools at the other end of the counter. Ray was a beefy man who invariably had enormous perspiration stains beneath the arms of his gray uniform shirt. Gary was smaller but muscular, with a bristling reddish mustache and lazy blue eyes. Both men enjoyed baiting Myra.

Ray rapped a hairy knuckle on the countertop. " 'Cause you're beautiful don't mean you can be slow," he said to Myra. "You ain't *that* beautiful."

Neither man looked at a menu.

"Usual," Gary said to Myra, not smiling.

Myra moved away from the counter and relayed the customary identical eggs, sausage and juice orders to the kitchen.

Ray sipped his coffee and pulled a face. "You'd think a ritzy place like this would have better coffee," he said to Gary.

"The prices ain't ritzy," Myra told him.

"Did you hear me ask about the prices?" Ray asked Gary.

Boston followed the sadistic banter silently. He despised people like Ray and Gary, who used their physical presence to intimidate. He felt, even secondhand and at a distance, the taint of shameful fear that Myra must feel. Then again, perhaps people like Myra didn't experience that uneasiness.

Myra took the orders from the serving shelf and set the plates on the counter before Ray and Gary. Silently, the deliverymen began to eat, preoccupied now that breakfast had arrived.

"Those two should choke on their food," Myra said to Boston.

He hoped the two men at the other end of the counter hadn't overheard. He didn't want to get pulled into their asinine repartee.

"People like that," Boston said softly, "and people like Harold Vish, wield too much power of one kind or another."

But Myra couldn't be lured into talking about Vish again. The mood of confidentiality had been broken.

Boston finished his coffee, which he regarded as quite good, and stood to go back upstairs. As he left a generous tip, he said, "Sometimes when a person burns the candle at both ends, it turns out to be a stick of dynamite that blows up unexpectedly."

But Myra hadn't understood what he meant. How was Arlo the dog? she asked.

Women liked Arlo.

107

18

"So it's Benson," Molly said, as she placed on Canby's desk the explosives manufacturers file she was delivering. Though it seemed longer, it had been less than seventy-two hours since the Morgell Trust Building destruction, and basic information was still accumulating.

"I hope so," Canby said.

"But you have doubts." Molly absently raised a hand to flip her long hair back behind her right shoulder. The portrait of the governor looked on approvingly, with even a touch of lechery.

"Maybe my doubts can be dispelled," Canby told her. "Benson's being brought in for questioning."

"Is he going to be charged?"

"No. Any lawyer would have him out within minutes. Then Benson would be uncooperative, on his guard and the recipient of expert legal advice. Not to mention that when the news media spread the story, he might by lynched."

"I'd like that," Molly said.

Canby was startled. "Why?"

"He tried to kill you," she said simply.

Not for the first time Canby glimpsed the flinty core that lay beneath her softness. She possessed, he realized, a certain boundless loyalty that could surface as savagery in defense of those she loved. Her hidden intensity excited him.

"We don't know for sure," he said, casting cool professionalism onto her passion and his own.

The deep, jewel-hard glitter was still in her eyes. "I believe that he did."

"You'd make a hell of a mama bear," Canby said, smiling.

"I guess that's a compliment, and I'd like to follow up on it but my phone is probably ringing itself crazy." She walked to the door, then turned. For a moment Canby was struck breathless by the arch of her body and the sculpture of her breasts beneath her plain white blouse. "Have you seen David Strother?" she asked.

"Not lately."

"He was by here earlier with his fiancee. A girl named Ann Ferris. He wanted to sit down with you and exchange information, mainly to find out more on the car-bombing incident."

Canby realized he hadn't kept Strother as informed as he'd promised. And since he'd decided to use Strother, he might as well use him to maximum effectiveness.

"I told him maybe the four of us could get together this evening for dinner at Durell's. That would force you to relax even while you were doing your job."

"All right," Canby said, but he was irritated by Molly's presumptuousness.

"You and Strother can decide on the time," she said, as if she sensed his mood and was slightly miffed herself. She didn't glance back as she went out the door.

Five minutes after she left, Mathews phoned.

"Benson's holed up in his house with a shotgun," he said. He sounded weary and eager at the same time.

"Christ," Canby said, with more disappointment than surprise. He could feel the whirl of events sweeping him toward a vortex of action where he had no real control. "I'm leaving for there now."

"The third is handling it, but they're waiting for you."

As Canby walked from his office, he wondered if Benson's resistance signified guilt or merely panic.

The block of near-vacant brick apartment buildings in the Bronx, interspersed with a few ramshackle single-family residences, was cordoned off and guarded by patrolmen from the third. Benson's small frame house was halfway down the block, a flat-roofed, faded green structure with black shutters and a kinked section of side guttering hanging down and out like an elbowed, weary arm. The entire house looked tired. This area of the Bronx looked tired. Several police cruisers were parked at angles to the house, doors open wide and being used as cover for the uniformed patrolmen crouching behind them. It was all very much like a textbook exercise to be graded at the academy.

Canby was met by Captain Bradner of the third. Jack Bradner was a tough cop who had risen through the ranks much as had Canby. The two men had worked together before and they got along well. In this instance, Canby's authority would supersede Bradner's, and Bradner would understand and cooperate.

"How long's he been in there, Jack?" Canby asked.

"A little less than an hour. He's already fired three rounds with a shotgun. Mostly to let us know he's got plenty of ammunition."

Canby and Bradner were standing several hundred feet up the street from where Benson was, beyond the line of angled police cars and in the shelter of an apartment building's concrete stoop.

Canby said, "Is he alone?"

Bradner nodded, his seamed face questioning, as if he were anxious to give the command for heavy fire to solve the situation within seconds. But his tiny brown eyes revealed nothing. Cop's eyes.

"Have you tried talking to him?" Canby asked.

Bradner nodded. "He answered the phone once but didn't talk, and he doesn't respond to the bullhorn. When the two detectives came to bring him in, he was polite, invited them inside, then pulled the shotgun on them, fired a shot in the air and ran them out." Bradner gave a wry, seam-deepening smile. "Their pride is hurt."

"Where did you phone from?"

"Right in there." Bradner pointed to a side entrance of the crumbling brick apartment building.

They went inside and up a short flight of rickety stairs to a first-floor apartment. Bradner had already made arrangements with the tenant, an obese black woman, and he led Canby directly to the phone. The sparsely furnished apartment gave off a stale, musty odor, mingled with the faintest suggestion of insecticide. From a bedroom doorway a small black boy of about six stared wide-eyed and silent at Canby, as if undecided whether to be hostile or friendly. A disc jockey was chattering from a radio somewhere, happy and glib and deep as a dime.

The phone was on an ancient red-enameled table in a hallway. Bradner gave Canby the number as Canby dialed.

Benson chose again not to answer. Canby could imagine the trapped fugitive, a husky, full-bearded man with a break-malformed nose, seated on the floor with his shotgun, impassively listening to his phone ring. Benson would maintain his impenetrable equanimity even if he hadn't the vaguest idea of what to do next. Yesteryear's rebel.

There was no time for a game of attrition. "I guess the next move is tear gas," Canby said.

"That's about it," Bradner agreed. "We wanted to wait till you got here."

They went outside, where Bradner could relay his instructions via walkie-talkie.

Canby nodded, and Bradner gave the order. Muted popping sounds drifted to them from down the street as tear gas canisters were fired through the frame house's windows. Canby had on civilian clothes. He drew his .38 revolver from its shoulder holster, and he and Bradner moved toward the Benson house, keeping as close as possible to the buildings on that side of the street.

A hundred yards away from the house, near an angled police cruiser, they stopped and stood poised, waiting. The three uniformed patrolmen crouched in the shelter of the cruiser were straining forward, their faces intent with determination and fear. The patrolman nearest Canby was holding a riot gun aimed at the house.

A grayish haze drifted lazily from the house's broken windows, like a manifestation of the sudden silence. No one came out.

"He probably went to the basement," Bradner said.

Canby nodded. "See if we can get a tear gas canister into that basement window just behind the porch."

Bradner relayed the instructions.

The first canister struck the frame side of the house with a wild plume of smoke that the breeze carried toward the back yard. The second struck the window casement and ricocheted inside the basement.

Bradner grunted. "That should do it."

But a full five minutes passed and still no one came out of the house. Canby had a decision to make. If the police opened fire, they could no doubt riddle the flimsy wood structure. But it was possible that there were explosives stored inside.

The alternative to ordering concentrated fire was to send in a detachment of men with gas masks to take Benson.

"I got six men with masks ready to go," Bradner said, anticipating Canby. "He's probably in there passed out."

"Send them," Canby said.

Within thirty seconds the six men were deployed around the house. Three were to enter the front way, three the back.

There was an abrupt, shrill whistle, and Canby watched the three grotesquely masked patrolmen assigned to storm the front of the house dash across the street and disappear behind some shrubbery in the front yard. Canby waited, expecting at any moment to hear gunfire.

There was only silence.

A few minutes later Bradner got the word over his walkie-talkie. The house was empty.

"He must have had some kind of escape route worked out," Bradner said, as he and Canby strode toward the besieged house. "Some sort of goddamn tunnel, maybe."

They entered the house, Canby still with his gun drawn. Most of the tear gas had been cleared out, but Canby still had to hold a handkerchief over his mouth and nose. His eyes were smarting and watering as if he'd been peeling onions. Uniformed patrolmen, some of them still wearing gas masks, were stomping through the house, yanking open closet doors, double-checking behind large pieces of threadbare furniture. The house was filthy with several months' accumulation of grime and debris. Empty beer cans and wine bottles lay among crumpled newspaper along one wall, on which was stapled a collage of aged political posters. A large modern oil painting hung unframed above the overturned sofa. Canby noted that the painting was an adroitly composed, disciplined piece of work that was at the same time somehow frighteningly wild.

He saw two men with gas masks go through a door that led to the basement stairs. He followed them. There was no way Benson could have escaped from the upper floor of the house.

The basement was filthier than the upstairs. The tear gas canister had torn a huge spider web as it crashed through the window, and the web hung in silky tatters, dotted with the dark husks of insects in the harsh light from the splintered opening in the dirt-smeared glass. There was a sagging workbench in one corner, loaded down with empty ceramic flowerpots. An old oil furnace against the far wall appeared

113

to be the only object offering substantial cover in the basement.

Both patrolmen checked out the basement with riot guns at the ready. Then they crossed the cement floor and one of them pulled a tarpaulin from a shrouded form near the base of the stairs to reveal a rusty, dented motorcycle.

Canby wandered away from the patrolmen, toward the other end of the basement. He'd noticed a large, boxlike attachment at the side of the oil furnace, and realized that it was a wood-burning addition to supplement the furnace and decrease heating costs. To the right of the furnace, in deep shadow, he saw what at first appeared to be a square piece of warped plywood leaning against the cement wall. He pulled on the plywood and found that it was actually the door of an ancient coal bin. The dim interior of the coal bin was stacked with firewood for the wood-burning auxiliary furnace.

Canby took a step into the coal bin, stood silently, and was about to withdraw when he heard a stirring beneath the firewood. His heart seemed to pump a spurt of paralyzing ice water through his veins. He thought of the blackened husks of insects in the spider web by the window, and of how the trapped insects must have felt at the unexpected approach of the spider.

Benson stood up from beneath the firewood.

He was taller than Canby remembered, eyes wide in his grit-blackened face. His denim shirt and Levis were wrinkled and torn on his muscular body, and through his dark beard his teeth showed in a startlingly white snarl that was almost a mad grin. His shotgun was in his right hand, pointing downward.

Canby automatically raised his revolver and aimed it at Benson. He could hear Benson's harsh breathing in the suffocating dimness. Now the snarl did turn to a grin. The barrel of the shotgun moved, slowly, not toward Canby.

"Don't!" Canby said hoarsely. He heard the movement of the uniformed patrolmen behind him in the basement. "God, please don't do it!"

In the sudden explosion and flash of the shotgun, Canby glimpsed the barrel held steady at the base of Benson's jaw, Benson's right arm extended rigidly to reach the trigger. Something warm and wet spattered Canby's forehead and left cheek. He backed out of the coal bin, staring down at the angry dark pattern of blood and matter on his shirt and pants. It was a composition wilder than the one hanging upstairs above the sofa.

Shouts. The thunder of feet descending the basement stairs.

Canby sat down on the grimy cement floor and vomited. Someone helped him up and he bent over and retched again, watching vomit splash onto the toes of his black shoes. He wiped his mouth with his handkerchief, spat off to the side and looked into the hardened, guarded face of Jack Bradner.

"He was in there." Canby motioned weakly with his right arm. "Under the firewood." He saw Bradner nod. "He turned the shotgun on himself."

Canby heard curses, then the choking sound of someone else vomiting.

"Who the fuck is gonna scrape up this mess?" a patrolman asked. At first Canby thought the man was referring to the vomit, and he felt a blaze of anger. Then he realized that the mess referred to was Benson. He began to tremble.

"C'mon, Dex," Bradner was saying, gently leading Canby toward the stairs. "Jesus! Enough's enough for one day."

Canby politely shook off Bradner's hand and leaned on the bottom of the banister. "Have the house searched," he told Bradner. "Let me know what you find. I'm going up to wash."

He climbed the stairs by himself.

19

Wilma Vish stepped out of the shower, then turned and gracefully bent her nude body to twist the chrome faucet handle to the off position. She stood in the steaming bathroom and began toweling herself dry, absently eyeing her slender, lithe body reflected in the misted full-length mirror.

The towel she was using was new, large and rough-textured. Wilma found the coarse material stimulating as she dried her back, moved the towel slowly around and massaged it gently against her small, firm breasts. She glanced down and saw her nipples become erect as she lowered the towel to her stomach and buttocks.

Harold hadn't made love to her in over two weeks, and yesterday she had stopped having her period. Wilma was always easily aroused immediately following her menstrual periods; she wondered if all women were. Raising one shapely leg and resting her bare foot on the edge of the washbasin, she sensuously ran the towel over her ankle, her calf, then her soft inner thigh. Sometimes during intercourse Harold had only to brush his fingertips along the insides of her thighs to prompt an orgasm.

Wilma wanted to open the bathroom door and go to Harold as she was, naked, stimulated and with reddened flesh still moist from the shower. But somehow she couldn't envision herself doing that, because she couldn't be sure of Harold's reaction. So she slipped into a long white terrycloth robe and left the bathroom eagerly yet hesitantly.

Harold Vish was in his study, seated at his typewriter and working on a review. The study was spartan and modern, with chrome-edged black leather furniture and a wide, kidney-shaped desk that had been the gift of a prominent theatrical agent. Wilma had never liked the desk. She thought it impractical and somewhat garish. But she had never mentioned her dislike to Harold.

Vish was seated motionless, shoulders lightly hunched, intently studying what he'd written that was still loosely furled in the typewriter. He had to be aware that Wilma had entered the study, but he didn't glance up.

Wilma sat on the edge of the desk, letting her robe part and feeling the coolness of the air-conditioned study wash over her.

Vish caught the expanse of flesh in the corner of his vision and looked up, momentarily startled. She saw the involuntary up-and-down flicker of his eyes and leaned toward him, aware of her own loud, irregular breathing.

Then he smiled with exaggerated indifference and turned back to his typewriter. "You know what they say about a time and a place," he told her, quickly pecking out a short sentence. He was having a particularly difficult time beginning his review of *Tropical Heat*.

"There are other maxims that might apply here," Wilma said, her passion supplanted by a tingling of anger at being rejected. Only a tingling, because perhaps Harold hadn't yet rejected her completely. She let the robe fall open farther so that both her breasts were bare.

"Such as?" Vish asked.

117

"Such as the maxim about the gift horse." As soon as she spoke the words, Wilma flushed in embarrassment at their self-deprecating implication.

But Vish only smiled, and that made Wilma more angry than if he'd openly insulted her or had made a tension-draining joke of her poorly chosen words.

Wilma pulled the white folds of her robe together and fastened them with a violent yank on the terrycloth belt. She stood erect and strode across the black-and-white shag carpet toward the door.

Vish watched her walk out without turning her head. She was actually not at all horsey, he reflected. She was a sensuous, attractive woman. It was the inner Wilma he'd become bored with to distraction. The bourgeois tastes, the jokes misunderstood or unnoticed, the serious points not taken, all had a cumulative effect that resulted in his not wanting to be long in the same room with Wilma. In the vernacular of horse aficionados, she was suitable only for a slow track.

Vish began his review for the third time: "Another in a long line of musical revivals done better the first time around, *Tropical Heat* . . ."

As he typed, he was smiling very slightly, thinking of his conversation with Wilma. And thinking of Helice.

The maxim he'd really had in mind was "Do unto others. . . ."

20

Canby drove directly from the ravaged Benson house to his apartment, where he showered, then put on his uniform. He went into the kitchen and began to make a sandwich, but realized with a wave of nausea that he couldn't yet eat. Even the beer he'd opened tasted flat and totally without flavor. Pouring the remainder of the beer into the sink, he dropped the empty can into the wastebasket, listened to its plaintive, metallic bounce and left the apartment.

Instead of going to his office at the seventeenth, Canby headed his new unmarked Pontiac sedan back toward the Benson house.

The scene of the shooting was deserted except for a single officer in a parked cruiser, guarding the house. Canby saw that there was an evidence seal on the front door. He yanked the steering wheel to swing his car in close to the parked cruiser.

"Where's Captain Bradner?" he asked, rolling down the air-conditioned Pontiac's window.

The man in the cruiser had to reach over and roll down his window on the passenger's side to hear. He was parked facing the wrong way, for an unobstructed view of the house.

Canby repeated his question, watching a glaze of respect come over the face of the young officer as he spotted Canby's blue captain's uniform. The officer told Canby that Bradner had returned to the third district precinct house.

Ten minutes later, Canby found Bradner seated at his desk in his office at the third. The precinct house was a converted aging brownstone row house with a ceiling stained by a chronically leaky roof. But Canby noticed that Bradner's office, though very much like his own, was the recipient of central air conditioning and was supplied with a worn green carpet.

Bradner made no mention of Canby's sickness at the death scene. He even tactfully ground out his odorous cigar in a large quartz ashtray that looked as if it had been pilfered from a posh hotel.

"Tell me we were lucky," Canby said.

Bradner shook his head, glancing down to make sure the cigar was dead. "I can't, Dex. There wasn't much in the Benson house but a lot of Marxist literature. The only weapon in the place was the shotgun Benson had. And there were three pounds of marijuana in the attic, in coffee cans."

Canby restrained himself from asking if the search had been thorough. There was no need to ask. Bradner knew his job. "No explosives?"

"None. And nothing that pertains to the Morgell Trust Building. Of course, not finding anything isn't conclusive one way or the other."

"I know," Canby said, "but it would have helped to find at least circumstantial evidence."

"Benson knew he was under suspicion. Maybe he figured he had to be careful about what was lying around the place."

"Benson wasn't the careful sort." The personality of the man was what bothered Canby all along. There was nothing in Dennis Benson's history to suggest he was the devious, painstaking "Jericho" type, the long-range planner. The only long-range goals Benson had sought were impersonal, political generalities. He was more the irrational firebrand than the meticulous planner.

"Maybe he had some stuff stashed in another locale," Bradner suggested.

"Why not in the attic with the marijuana?"

"You got me," Bradner said, unconsciously picking up the dead cigar from the ashtray and holding it between thumb and forefinger. "Who knows for sure? Guys like Benson can't even figure themselves out."

Mayor Danner punched the button that activated the recorder on his telephone line. Then he picked up the receiver of his desk phone. The caller had maintained that the call concerned the Morgell Trust Building destruction and per instructions was put through to the mayor immediately.

The voice on the phone was high-pitched, mechanically distorted, without sex or distinction. Its inhuman quality caused a trickle of cold to play along Danner's spine.

The mayor listened carefully to his instructions. If Dennis Benson had indeed been Jericho, this was his confederate.

But no mention was made of Benson as the strident distorted voice laid down in concise manner the rules of the game. The money was to be kept at the mayor's sister's plush townhouse on East Eighty-seventh Street, where the phone would ring with further instructions. The mayor was advised that these instructions must be carried out on a moment's notice.

"I'm having difficulty raising all the money," Danner said, which was true. "I can get it, I'm sure. But a million dollars takes time."

"I know that," the shrill voice replied with a touch of impatience. "I intend to grant you more time. But this second segment of time will be your last. Three more days. Be ready to part with *all* the money after three more days."

Mayor Danner started to reply that he'd be ready, but the receiver clicked, then buzzed in his ear, as the caller hung up.

Danner replaced the receiver quickly, as if it had suddenly become something repulsive. He was sweating. After Benson's death, some of the pressure had been lifted. But only some. Danner had never been as positive as the news media that Benson was the bomber. In politics and in life, few permanent solutions proved to be so direct and uncomplicated.

The air in the office seemed unnaturally heavy to Danner, as if the room were pressurized. Traffic noises filtered in from outside, the faint bass hum of a bus, a driver impatiently leaning on his car's horn to vent his anger at what he couldn't control. Sounds of Danner's city, the city of so much love and hate, splendor and squalor.

And now a city inhibited by the fear of its greatness unexpectedly crashing down into its streets. Though still in masses, there must be somewhat fewer tourists, fewer people on the sidewalks, in the towering office buildings, the restaurants and theaters. The economic effect of fear would soon become another major concern for a city whose lifeblood consisted of gushing green currency, a city where money and time and their relationship dominated.

Three more days . . . The final segment of time before unprecedented horror for that city.

Thorpe had told Danner there might be an extension on the time limit. It wasn't unusual for an extortionist to grant an almost impossible initial deadline so the victim would react in panic-stricken haste and think of nothing but cooperation. The second segment of time was to ensure that the victim, now cooperative, actually had opportunity to carry out instructions fully. Thus the most important part of the game, transferring the money, would go smoothly. There would be no more extensions.

Danner knew he should phone Thorpe and report the conversation with the extortionist as soon as possible. Thorpe had been so sure about Benson, had used the man's death to assuage the media, like tossing meat to following wolves. Danner hoped Thorpe was smart enough to know his job as

122

police commissioner was on the line. And he hoped Thorpe had been smart enough to choose the right man to head the investigation. In something like the Morgell Trust case, the machinery of the law would be impotent without a certain type of exceptional man at the controls. That sort of man was never easy to find.

The mayor reached again for the telephone, then he hesitated. His hand moved to the left and pressed a button on his walnut intercom console. Daily reassurances from Thorpe were not enough.

"Get Police Captain Dexter P. Canby over here to see me," he said to his secretary.

21

Ann Ferris slipped a smaller lens onto her 35-millimeter Pentax camera and adjusted the focus. As Strother stood at the dresser mirror buttoning his shirt, the camera clicked and whirred three times in quick succession as Ann caught his candid motions and the automatic winder advanced the film.

Ann was a professional photographer for an advertising agency on East Fortieth. But she also did free-lance work for various magazines, and like many free-lancers was seldom without her camera. Strother was so used to her idly capturing his movements on film that he hardly noticed. Nine out of ten of the developed photographs she would throw away. Later she would throw away nine of the ten she'd kept. Ann was a dedicated professional, a perfectionist, which was why she was one of the best at her job.

She replaced the Pentax in its leather shock case and slung the case by its strap on a chair near the bed. She and Strother had just finished making love, and she stretched long bare arms over her head and sighed. Strother glanced at her reflection in the dresser mirror as he tucked in his shirt.

Ann was tall and slender, once a photographers' model herself, with dark flowing hair, dark eyes and a gaunt-cheeked, starved and cool expression that might have helped her become a successful fashion model.

Ten years ago, at twenty-five, she had decided she didn't want to become a model. She didn't want to be merchandised; if it was fine with other women, it wasn't with her. For a while she'd become fervently active in the women's liberation movement, and had published a book of photographs illustrating the inferior roles society had imposed upon females. But over the years, as the movement became more and more militant, her interest had waned. After the Houston convention fiasco, she'd become inactive in the organized liberation movement and was now only a concerned observer. But her interest in her own independence was as burning as ever.

Strother walked to her and kissed her cheek. "Why don't you get dressed," he said, "and we'll go out and forage a meal."

Ann shook her head in pretended scorn. "Food and sex often occupy your thoughts, don't they, David?"

"Not in that order." He stared frankly at her tanned, angular nudity. "And not simultaneously. Your ribs are showing."

"Then I suppose it is time for food."

Strother walked into the living room and waited for Ann to dress. He picked up his highball glass and drained the icy remains of the drink. He'd needed the past hour with Ann. It was the only time since he had heard about the Morgell Trust Building's destruction that he'd really thought about anything unconnected to that calamity. Concern for the case still permeated his consciousness, but now he somehow felt more in control of things. At the core of his mind was the precious still kernel of peacefulness that Ann always left with him.

Strother had thought briefly that the death of Benson might

have solved everyone's problems. But there was too much about Benson that didn't fit the mold of the man they were seeking. Most importantly, there was nothing in Benson's past to suggest he could have acquired the expertise to bring down the Morgell Trust Building.

When Strother had talked to Canby and learned the police captain's similar thoughts on the subject, and that a search of Benson's house had divulged nothing to indicate his involvement in the bombing, Strother had become even more depressed. If Benson was innocent and had shot himself out of panic or under the influence of drugs, his death would prove only a tragic hindrance in solving the case in time.

Ann stood in the doorway, outfitted in tan slacks, an oversized pink shirt and a dangling gold chain necklace that a smaller woman would never have gotten away with wearing. On Ann, everything always appeared to be precisely the thing to wear at the moment.

"Marriage," she said.

"Just lunch for now," Strother told her, somewhat puzzled.

Ann sat on the sofa with her long legs crossed. "I mean, maybe that's something to consider in this Morgell Trust Building case. You've been concentrating on the area's demolition experts, and every one of them is a man."

"It's not an occupation many women seem to want to pursue."

"But what about the wives of some of these demolition experts? Surely over the course of years a wife can learn a lot about her husband's occupation, probably even enough to achieve a reasonable degree of proficiency."

Strother stared thoughtfully at her. "You're suggesting that Jericho is a woman?"

"It's a possibility. Granted, dynamite is macho, but don't let the fact that demolition is usually a man's game deceive you."

Strother walked to the window, hands on hips. The muted sounds of traffic rushed up at him. "One of the wives—"

"Or ex-wives."

He turned and grinned at Ann, the light from the window making the grin appear crooked.

She shrugged. "I hope you don't feel threatened."

Strother ignored her and walked in long strides to the telephone. He dialed the seventeenth precinct's number and was told that Canby wasn't in. He had his call switched to Molly Garrity's extension.

Canby would be gone for about an hour, Molly told Strother. He had been summoned to the mayor's office. She didn't know why.

22

Mayor Danner finished telling Canby about the extortionist's phone call and sat back in his upholstered desk chair. He touched the flame of a souvenir-of-New York lighter to the bowl of a briar pipe.

"We know for sure now that Benson wasn't Jericho," Canby said, realizing that he'd never seen Mayor Danner smoke in public.

"Or we know that he was only one of the extortionists."

"There's that possibility," Canby conceded.

The mayor gazed at Canby over the glowing bowl of the pipe. "You never were convinced of Benson's involvement."

Canby was surprised by Danner's insight. "No, I wasn't."

"Because there was too much that wouldn't fit?"

Canby relaxed in his velvet-cushioned chair and shook his head. "There were some aspects of the case that didn't fit, but then there always are. It was more the way things fit, either too snug or too loose. Call my conviction that Benson had nothing to do with the Morgell Trust bombing a hunch if you want to, but after enough years and enough lumps a cop develops instincts he learns to trust."

"I don't discount the value of your instincts," Danner said, exhaling a great cloud of noxious smoke. He liked Canby's reference to himself as a "cop." "And Commissioner Thorpe believes in your intuition; that's why you were put in charge of the investigation. There are plenty of men in the department who are qualified, men with more rank and motivation."

"Motivation?"

Danner smiled, set the pipe in an ashtray at a careful angle so it would continue burning evenly and fouling the air. "Political motivation, Captain Canby. Did the political implications of the case escape you?"

"I was more concerned with escaping them, sir." Canby glanced around at the spacious, posh office, with its deep pile carpet and heavy walnut-framed portraits. "I don't care about the political implications. At least not the positive ones."

Danner appeared puzzled.

"I don't care about any political gain that comes out of my helping to break this case," Canby explained. "On the other hand, I don't think I should be crucified if the case doesn't break. But I know I will be."

"Negative implications indeed," Danner said, "and very real. For both of us. That's why I wanted to talk with you personally, to affirm my belief in Thorpe's judgment. I'm satisfied with you, Captain Canby."

At this point, Canby thought, it hardly makes a difference. But he remained silent.

Danner began tracing meaningless designs on the shiny desk top with the tip of a thick forefinger. "What now, Captain?"

Canby rose from the small chair, paced a few steps, then stood holding his uniform cap lightly with both hands. "Do we still intend to pay?"

Danner nodded. "That one is my decision."

Canby thought, Thank God for that. "For now, we should obey all the instructions," he said. "It's the only safe way to conduct ourselves, and whoever we're after is less likely to be on guard if we appear to be cooperating fully."

Danner leaned forward with his elbows on the desk top. It was a long-practiced gesture to signify the importance of what he was about to say, but in this instance it was unconscious and genuine. "I intend to cooperate fully, Captain Canby, one way or the other. If whoever is doing this gets away with the money, so be it."

"As you said, sir, that one's your decision."

"It's the only way I can go, I discover."

Canby looked into the mayor's shrewd eyes and tried to decide if Danner was playing politics. He decided the mayor was sincere, and maybe even a bit surprised at his own sincerity.

"I understand, your honor." Canby realized that he was impressed by the mayor. It was no wonder the man had been elected. But Canby did understand. What they'd been caught up in transcended politics, whether anyone liked it or not, or admitted it or not.

"I have a meeting with some of the bankers involved in granting the city a loan. There's no doubt I can get the money; I have the power to make it worth their while. But I'll keep you personally apprised."

"How soon do you think you can have the money?"

"Well within the three-day limit, possibly by tomorrow morning. If it had come to push and shove, I could have raised it by this afternoon."

Canby didn't doubt it.

"I'll see that the money gets to my sister's residence as soon as possible."

"I'll have a guard posted there when it arrives, sir. I'm sure Jericho expects that, since he didn't demand otherwise. We have to be careful to stay within the specified and unspecified rules."

"Rules . . . Is that how whoever is doing this sees it? As some sort of horrible game?"

"It isn't horrible in his eyes, sir. Only potentially profitable. And to such a wild degree that he feels almost any action is justifiable."

Danner wiped a hand slowly across his broad forehead, as if to smooth away any creases of worry. "We'll figure out how to deal with him," he said. "Hell, I've even figured out how to deal with Republicans."

"Then this should be a pleasure," Canby said.

Danner looked up sharply, surprised at Canby's flash of humor. A smile shadowed his lips. "Hardly a pleasure," he said. The smile was gone. "I'm going to give my aides instructions to put through your phone calls to me immediately, even if I'm out of this office."

"That's a good idea, sir. We might get down to counting minutes."

"I'm reasonably sure that I can rely on you, Captain. I want you to know you can rely on me."

"I'm sure I can, sir."

"I mean beyond the realm of politics," Danner said. "If you need me for some course of action that's politically damaging, even politically suicidal, I'm willing. I don't want there to be any hesitancy about doing the right thing here because of political considerations."

"I see." Canby studied the mayor's open Irish face with its contrasting uncompromising mouth and chin. He believed the mayor as completely as he could believe a politician.

"There are those who don't grasp the scope of what's going on," Danner said.

"Yes, sir, that's true."

Mayor Danner stood. "To keep things aboveboard, I'll inform Thorpe that I've given you instructions to deal with me direct. You needn't worry about him thinking you've gone behind his back." The all-Irish smile. "You don't have any choice."

131

As the mayor walked with him to the office door, Canby wondered if Thorpe was one of those whose grasp of the situation the mayor doubted. Canby thought that was possible.

Mayor Danner's parting handshake was lengthy and very firm, somewhat moist. Not at all a politician's handshake.

As Canby was walking along the cork-floored corridor outside the mayor's office, he was approached by a tall, square-featured man who moved with the easy, offhand grace of a born athlete. Canby knew who the man was.

"Captain Canby, I'm Carl Gaines," the man told him. "The mayor's administrative assistant." They shook hands. "I know you've just seen Mayor Danner, and I want to convey to you the willingness of everyone in the mayor's employ."

"Willingness to do what?"

"To cooperate in the Morgell Trust Building investigation, in whatever way necessary."

"I appreciate that, Mr. Gaines."

A gaunt black man with a goatee, accompanied by a graying, flawlessly groomed white man in a vested suit, stepped around them and walked on, talking in low monotones. Gaines waited until they were around the corner before speaking again.

"I mean, Captain Canby, that some of us will cooperate regardless of circumstances. Any circumstances." The squarish features were serious, wary. A bead of perspiration trickled along Gaines's jaw.

Canby stared at him. "I see. I'll remember that, Mr. Gaines."

Gaines smiled at him before turning and walking to a door halfway down the hall. As the mayor's assistant stepped out of sight, Canby decided that the door must lead to a suite of offices adjacent to the mayor's office. Apparently Gaines had his own private entrance.

Canby walked toward the elevators. No doubt Gaines was of the opinion that there were those who failed to grasp the political scope of the situation.

The Gaineses of the world frightened Canby.

23

Harvey Metzger, the Beymer Building's maintenance chief, took the service elevator to the twenty-second floor and walked along the hall toward apartment 22E. The apartment was vacant and being redecorated, and he wanted to check on the subcontractor he'd hired to paint and paper the walls.

He used his passkey on 22E and entered, hearing the raucous, flat rhythm of a rock song on a radio.

A young man in white overalls was balanced on a paint-smeared stepladder, skillfully scraping paint spots from the windowpane with a razor blade. The entry hall and living room were finished except for the carpet being cleaned. Metzger nodded to the young painter, looked around and was satisfied.

Stepping over the small portable radio, which was blaring as if in pain, he went into the master bedroom and saw another painter applying paint to the far wall with a roller.

"We'll be done today easy, Mr. Metzger," the painter said, maneuvering the roller perilously close to the stained wood-work.

"Fine," Metzger said, smiling. But he was thinking that ten years ago he could have gotten the job finished in half the time for a third of the cost. The world had changed.

"I'll arrange for the carpet man to come in tomorrow to steam-clean," Metzger said. He made a point of surveying the room. "It's looking fine." It would serve no purpose to insult the painter, and in truth the job was neat even if it had taken too long.

Metzger left the apartment and walked back toward the elevator, noticing that the carpet in the hall had reached the point where the practiced eye could detect signs of wear. Next week he would broach the matter of a new carpet to Remmer Properties, owner and manager of the Beymer Building.

As he descended in the service elevator, Metzger unconsciously leaned down and picked up a bent nail. He had been maintenance chief at the building for nine years, and he felt a sense of possession now that accompanied his responsibility to deal with stopped drains, electrical failures and the scores of other minor afflictions that plagued any large Manhattan building.

When Metzger stepped out of the elevator, he was in the subbasement. Six years ago, when an exclusive luggage shop had opened in the Beymer lobby, he had talked Remmer Properties into constructing the subbasement. A man from Remmer had come out, and with slow, irrefutable logic, Metzger had convinced him that storage of the luggage shop's stock eliminated needed room at the basement level and might even cause the building to fail to pass the city's fire inspection. Since the storage area was included in the luggage shop's lease, the small subbasement had been constructed.

But within a year the luggage shop had gone out of business. Metzger had talked again with his employer, and after a downward adjustment of salary, he was allowed to install a small but comfortable apartment for himself in the subbasement.

At first he'd spent only two or three nights a week in the

apartment, saving in transportation costs and time lost what he'd given up in salary. And the apartment served as an office as well as a convenient sanctuary.

Then, four years ago, when his wife of thirty years had left him to return to her family in Germany, Metzger had moved into the apartment on a permanent basis.

He entered the apartment now, crossed to a large vinyl-covered recliner and sat down. He was almost sixty-three years old, and, while still hearty, he knew he should use his time wisely and enjoy himself. Life owed him that.

Metzger's principal pleasure was working on his model sailing ships. The shelves and tables of the small apartment were adorned with dozens of such ships, small and graceful sloops, the larger three-masted cargo ships of the late eighteen hundreds, Spanish armed galleons of Drake's era. Each model was an obvious creation of pride and painstaking hours of work.

When he was in his early twenties, Metzger had spent three years in the U.S. Navy, leaving him with a distaste for authority and a love for the sea and sailing ships. But only sailing ships, not the steamships of unbending discipline and endless, mindless routine. Metzger would spend long hours in his apartment gazing at the detailed, thoroughly wrought model ships around him, imagining himself sailing warm waters and putting in at exotic ports where a younger Metzger found adventure and the love of faithful women.

Metzger was a man who'd had his way with women. He hadn't always been bent with arthritis, and his complexion hadn't always been its present sallow, almost yellowish cast.

He crossed to a card table near a large lamp, where he was building his latest model, a nineteenth-century English sloop, and sat down. He didn't like to compare his younger days with the present.

The telephone rang, and Metzger dropped his carving tool and lifted the receiver.

The caller identified herself as Mrs. Wexley, 17B. Her garbage disposal wasn't working, but she didn't want it repaired now because she would soon have guests. She just wanted Metzger to know about it.

Metzger thanked her for calling and told her he'd look at the disposal in the morning if that was convenient. Morning was fine with Mrs. Wexley, and while he was there he could check the left front burner on the kitchen range. Lately it had refused to come on while the oven was in use. Metzger assured her that he'd check the range and hung up the phone.

Then he bent over the intricate three-master and dreamed of sailing.

24

"Why don't you ease up, Dex? Please?"

Canby was in his office, going over the demolition experts file before him on his desk. Molly, off duty, was seated in a chair near the door, staring with worried appraisal at him.

The desk lamp cast a deep-shadowed yellow glow over Canby's features, highlighting the ravages of constant tension and adding years to his face. The four days since the Morgell Trust tragedy had accelerated his aging process.

"You can delegate some of your authority," Molly went on, when he didn't answer. "There's no reason you have to do everything yourself."

Canby knew she didn't understand that in a situation like this he *did* have to do much of the work himself. That was how the responsibility weighed on you: you feared for anyone who might make the crucial mistake you wouldn't have made in his or her place. "Civic duty" had always been, if not an empty phrase, an ambiguous one to Canby. Now he knew that despite its meaningless mouthings by scores of public officials, despite its countless uses as a candidate's catchall generality, it worked, it demanded, it was there. Civic duty. Canby knew how the mayor must feel, a politician whose politics had carried him beyond Machiavellian maneuvering to direct life-and-death decision making under the pressure of fleeting time.

"Strother had an idea," Canby said. "A good one. We're looking into the possibility that one of the demolition men's wives picked up enough knowledge of her husband's trade to have brought down the Morgell Trust Building."

Molly smoothed back her red hair and crossed her legs. The yellowish light that cast years on Canby somehow made her appear younger. "That doesn't seem likely to me, Dex. Such specialized knowledge." Her look was one of possessive concern. "I think you're exhausted—"

"But it's possible."

"Percentage-wise, not much isn't. But the percentages are so small. Why don't you come away and have a few drinks and some supper?"

"Things need to be done yet tonight. Strother's already checking on some of the wives, and information is coming in all the time from the rest of the men in the field."

Molly sighed, not in exasperation but in resignation. "It's become a solemn sort of game. As tragic and potent as the situation is, that's what it's become to you."

Canby's voice was level. "No, but it is like a game in some respects. There are moves that have to be made. As soon as possible."

Molly stood up. He thought she was going to leave.

Instead she walked over and kissed him on the forehead. Her lips were cool, rigid with her yearning. "You're special, do you know that?"

"Of course." He patted her hip and turned his attention to the file. He felt a bit cheap about making a joke of what she'd said; he knew she'd meant it and that he was fortunate.

"Can I help?" she asked.

"You can stay here if you'd like. Help organize the information as it comes in." He glanced up at her and smiled. "And make everything easier by being around. You have that effect on me."

She kissed him again, lightly this time, then moved away. "You know I'm always with you, Dex."

He knew.

By morning they were almost out of wives.

None of the demolition men's spouses had proved to be even slightly suspicious. The ones who might have succeeded in obtaining specialized knowledge of demolition had established alibis of one kind or another. If they had been married long enough to their husbands to pick up the necessary knowledge, the couple usually was from another area and had relocated here. Or the physical possibilities, their past or psychological profiles, made them even more unlikely as suspects than had been the unfortunate Benson.

Now the operation was reduced to checking the divorcees and widows, but most of them had either relocated or remarried and proved unpromising as suspects.

Strother had asked Canby if he might do some personal checking, since the area of investigation was his idea, and Canby had given him permission. There was no reason not to, as deeply involved as the architect was now. As matters stood, before long Strother wouldn't be so eager to claim the idea as his own. And Canby wouldn't be at all eager to claim Strother.

Molly had stayed with Canby, resisting his occasional urgings for her to go home and sleep. Until at 3:30 A.M. she did fall asleep in one of the high-backed wooden chairs near Canby's desk. It amazed Canby that anyone could sleep in that chair.

She agreed then to go home. As she stood up, eyelids drooping with fatigue, she murmured to Canby again that she loved him.

"That's one of the few things in my life I don't doubt," Canby told her. And again that love was confirmed in the

140

weary eyes gazing up at him. He bent and kissed her. "I'll call for a cab," he said.

She smiled, nodded and sat down again.

Canby's breathing quickened as he looked at her. She had inundated his life and quickly become his strength and weakness. He pulled the phone across the desk toward him and dialed.

Hour after hour, via teletype, phone and personal report, information, discouraging as it was, continued to filter into the seventeenth. But if it included anything pertinent, Canby couldn't discern it.

25

Strother turned his car onto Garret Street in Queens, in the old neighborhood where Dimitri Kivas had lived. Despite the lingering heat, there were several people out on the sidewalks or sitting on the front stoops of the old but neat brick flats. Most of those milling about were teen-agers or young children, though Strother noted an old man and a hunchbacked gray-haired woman walking hand in hand, the woman trailing the man slightly like an admonishing pale shadow. In the mouth of a narrow alley, a shirtless man smoking a cigar was dutifully polishing an aging station wagon as if performing a god-appeasing ritual.

The sun was almost down, and the dark rectangular shadows of the nearly identical buildings crisscrossed the street symmetrically, like spaces marked out on a game board. Strother parked in front of the building he'd visited earlier that week. He felt conspicuous as he locked his car, then walked in through the building's pneumatically hissing vestibule door, but he realized that the sounds of the street were unchanged by his presence.

On the first floor, amid that same curious smell of pungent, mingled cooking odors, he knocked on the door to the flat of the super.

When she opened the door, immediately the odors of her flat overwhelmed the hall odors. The smell of cat urine was predominant. The old woman recognized Strother after a moment's hesitation and smiled. It was a bright smile despite being timeworn and blatantly eager.

"You talked to me earlier about Mr. Kivas," the woman said.

"That's right, Mrs. . . . ?"

"Lappon," the old woman said. "I forgot to introduce myself last time. You're Mr. Strother."

Strother nodded, somewhat startled that she'd remembered his name. Mrs. Lappon stepped back to allow him to enter her dim apartment. The huge gray cat was curled in a corner of the sagging sofa and eyed him with a feline combination of wariness and indifference.

Strother sat in an aged velvet chair that creaked under his weight as if in rapture. The old woman sat next to the cat on the sofa.

"I need to know more about Dimitri Kivas," Strother told her. "And his wife. It's important."

She looked at him in a faintly quizzical manner, her almost nonexistent gray eyebrows arched on her delicate parchment forehead. "But he's dead."

"Is his wife still living?"

Mrs. Lappon shrugged and began stroking the gray cat.

"She must be," Strother said in answer to his own question. "Kivas was a comparatively young man when he died. Was his wife about his age?"

"About. Yes. Her name was Vera. Pretty. . . ."

Strother didn't know if Mrs. Lappon meant the cat or Mrs. Kivas. "Could you describe her?" he asked.

143

"Pretty. A woman who kept a clean house but could not cook."

"But what did she *look* like?" Strother was fighting to control his frustration.

"Dark hair, small, quick of eye and smart. Smart, that one."

Strother's interest heightened. "Smart? Why do you say that, Mrs. Lappon?"

"Vera would talk to the other women of the neighborhood, but always she remained apart in some way. And often, if there was an argument, she would settle it with a word, as if she were in the company of children and could no longer bear to hear them bicker. But I can say little evil about a woman who so loved her husband."

"She and Dimitri were unusually close?"

"Vera stayed with him both in body and spirit while he was dying. For that she earned everyone's respect. Then, when he died, she left. Within a week she gave her notice here and moved out."

"Moved where?"

"She did not say. No one asked. There was no one in the neighborhood that close to her."

"Her name isn't in the phone directory, or anywhere else I've looked. Did you hear of her remarrying?"

"No. I don't believe Vera would remarry. At least not for a long time. . . . She was that sort of woman. There still *are* some."

"Was she interested at all in her husband's work?"

"His work?" Mrs. Lappon moved her hand and the cat rumbled softly with pleasure. "Vera and Dimitri were interested in each other, but I never heard her talk of her husband's work. Still, I am sure she was interested in everything about Dimitri. They were both happy and lucky. Such things have a way of ending prematurely, I've noticed."

Strother wondered if the old woman was talking about something in her own past. But there was no pain in the faded eyes, only recollection.

"I went to his funeral," Mrs. Lappon said, as if the memory

gave her some subtle pleasure. "We were of the same church."

"Did Mrs. Kivas also belong to the church?"

"Yes. It is of the Herras religion."

Strother vaguely remembered once reading something about the Herras religion but couldn't remember what.

"Perhaps the minister would know where Mrs. Kivas moved," he suggested.

Mrs. Lappon stroked the cat and nodded, in agreement that it was possible. She said, "We have no ministers in the Herras faith, they are called sayers."

Another thought struck Strother. "Were there very many people at the Kivas funeral?" Possibly a friend of the family who attended would know Vera's whereabouts if the "sayer" didn't.

Mrs. Lappon seemed to be straining to recall. The fine lines of her face deepened. "There were some from where Mr. Kivas worked. I think perhaps a brother of Vera Kivas, and a few people from the church and the neighborhood. It's been years ago—"

"I know." Strother stood. The cat purred. "I appreciate your help, Mrs. Lappon. One more thing: Could you tell me where to find the Herras church the Kivases attended?"

"Of course. It's here in the neighborhood. On Tower Street, around the corner five blocks north."

Strother thanked her again, assured her that he could manage his own way out and that she should stay seated. The cat stared at him with aloof contempt as he left.

Garret Street was still active, muted in the gathering dusk. Strother decided to walk the five blocks to the Herras church. He wasn't sure if he had a hunch that he was onto something, or if what he felt was simply the culmination of his desperation. On his first visit, Mrs. Lappon had mentioned that the Kivases had lived in the building for several years. It seemed unusual that in that length of time Vera Kivas wouldn't have made enough acquaintances to bother informing someone of her future whereabouts after her husband's death. Strother was getting more curious all the time about Vera Kivas.

145

* * *

The Herras church was a converted four-family flat that resembled most of the other brick buildings on Tower Street. From atop its crumbling façade rose a graceful cross, and one of its front windows had been replaced by an ornate stained-glass depiction of the crucifixion. Several pigeons strutted aimlessly about on the parapet, above where their droppings had marked the stained glass.

When Strother entered the building he found that most of the first floor had been made into one large room. Rows of uncomfortable-appearing pews occupied the center of the church, facing an altar edged in dark-veined marble. The carpeting was deep red and worn; the walls were paneled half-way up, then painted a faded gray color like that of an overcast sky. Patterns of light fell across the pews and the carpet and walls, tinted delicately by the pastels of the stained-glass front window. Strother saw a flight of stairs behind and to the left of the altar and guessed that the sayer must live in the flat's upper story.

But a door near the base of the stairs opened and a tall man in a black suit and white collar with a black string tie stepped out and nodded to Strother. He walked slowly toward Strother with a steady yet uneven gait, as if the cells of his body remembered great pain, and smiled questioningly. Now that he was nearer, Strother could see that his black hair was touched with not gray but white, and his lean, dark face was deeply lined. His brown eyes were compassionate but alert.

"I am Mr. Jamess," he said.

Strother shook a strong, dry hand. "You are the sayer of this church, I was told. Is that roughly the equivalent of a minister?"

"Roughly," Jamess said with a nod. "But we are a religion without leaders other than God. The Herras religion began centuries ago in southern Europe and embraces many nationalities. All equal in the Lord's eyes."

"And what is the nationality of most of the people in this parish—neighborhood?"

146

Jamess shrugged. "There are many nationalities here—Greek, Italian, Spanish—many who follow the teachings of God and the Herras." The sayer raised a bony forefinger and asked Strother to wait a minute. He disappeared through the doorway from which he'd emerged and returned shortly with a handful of pamphlets and mimeographed sheets, which he gave to Strother. The doctrine and history of the Herras faith, he explained. A chronicle of survival.

Strother thanked him and asked, "Do you remember Dimitri and Vera Kivas? They attended church here."

"I remember," Jamess said. Most of the teeth on one side of his mouth appeared to be missing, giving his slender face an oddly lopsided figuration when he talked. "Dimitri Kivas died some years ago. I read the mass at his funeral."

"Do you know where I might find his widow?"

"Vera Kivas? No, she moved away shortly after her husband's death. She didn't mention where she was going."

"Not even to her fellow congregation members? Isn't that unusual?"

"With people, Mr. Strother, the unusual is the usual. I saw no need to question her."

"Of course not. Can you remember if she had any particularly close friends from the church?"

The sayer caressed his narrow skull with a slender hand. "There was Miss Bellas," he said after a pause. "Nora Bellas. She is still of the faith but the man she married is not. They live on a small farm not too distant from the city. I don't know exactly where. Her married name is . . . Holden, I believe. She might know where you can reach Vera Kivas."

"Can you describe Vera Kivas? It would help, in case Mrs. Holden doesn't know where to locate her."

Again the lean fingers pressed into coarse black hair grained with white at the side of Jamess's head. "Vera was an attractive woman. Dark hair, slender, graceful. Her features were regular. I do not remember the color of her eyes. What I remember most is her devotion to her husband."

Strother thanked Jamess and gave him a telephone number

to call in case he remembered something more about Vera Kivas. Then he left the church.

Outside on Tower Street, he realized he was still clutching the handful of pamphlets Jamess had given him. After folding the church literature, he stuffed it into his hip pocket. He could read it later. Right now he wanted to talk to Canby so the Police Department could find the exact location of the Holden farm as soon as possible.

From inside the church came the faint sound of recorded music, the plucking of a simple stringed instrument the name of which eluded Strother. The pigeons on the parapet flapped and cooed, breaking the pattern of the music, seemingly ending it.

Strother walked quickly back toward his car, the rhythm of his footfalls on the sidewalk echoing faintly ahead of him as if drawing him on.

26

Wilma Vish recognized the cloyingly alluring scent of Helice Gorham's perfume. The imported perfume was expensive; it was distinct; and Helice wore too much of it too often. Wilma detected the lilac scent now as she stood before her husband's open closet.

It didn't take her long to find the source of the perfume scent. Harold's brown vest. He'd forgotten to drop it off at the cleaners with the rest of the brown suit.

Ordinarily, when Wilma came across such circumstantial evidence of Harold's infidelity she ignored it, blocking out the dart of pain and fear so that she wouldn't have to cope with what she was sure was true. Harold was conducting a not very discreet affair with Helice Gorham. Others in the building had to know, or at least suspect, that the two were lovers.

If Harold had to maintain an extramarital affair, why did it have to be here, in the building where they lived? Was there something in their marriage that caused him to want to hurt her as much as possible?

As she stood holding the soft summer-weight suit vest and the sweetness of the perfume wafted about her, Wilma's pain of betrayal became a slowly building anger. Harold wasn't entirely to blame. Helice Gorham, of the sophisticated manner and expensive stylish clothes, knew that he was married. Wilma wondered, Would Helice be so imperturbable if the wronged wife knocked on her door and confronted her with what she knew? For a dangerous, seething moment, Wilma considered finding out the answer to that question.

It was a temptation that Wilma resisted. Not that she hadn't the courage. It was just that right now she wasn't sure what she should do. That which she *should* do had always dominated Wilma's thoughts and actions.

She glanced at the imitation-pearl clock near the bed and saw that the evening had slipped away to ten o'clock. Where was Harold now? At a critics' meeting where he said he was going? Or was he five floors below with Helice Gorham?

Wilma replaced the brown vest on its hanger and slid the closet door closed, sharply.

"And where does little Wilma think you are at this moment?" Helice asked Harold Vish. They were in Helice's apartment. Vish was wearing nothing but a red velour robe. Helice had on an expensive and diaphanous pink French gown.

"I told her I had a meeting," Vish said, sipping his scotch. "Which in a sense is true."

Helice curled long legs beneath her in the angle of a sofa corner. She appeared thoughtful. "Why is it, Harold, that decadence attracts you?"

"It's you who attracts me."

"I know."

"Since you insist on being philosophical," Vish said, "I simply find what you call decadence fun. Contrary to public misconception, there's always something fresh and unique in good old decadence. The Romans knew a thing or two."

"Hmm," Helice reflected. She rose from the sofa and

crossed the room to where her drink was sitting on a glass-topped table.

Vish watched the movement of her lean hips beneath the sheer gown, the play of lamplight on her smooth bare shoulders. The tightening sensation in his groin grew from pleasure to a need almost unbearable.

"You are the most blatant bastard I ever met," Helice told him, picking up her glass. "With the most perverse instinct for sensational destruction."

"I doubt that."

When she passed near him, on the way back to the sofa, he stood and blocked her way. She stared up into his face, amusement and something else sparking her blue eyes.

"I really don't care what you are," she said.

Vish knew that was true. His hands went to her, found the flare of her hips beneath the sheer gown and squeezed hard enough to bring a wince of pain to her features.

He said softly, "Bedroom, bitch."

She smiled and walked ahead of him.

Helice occasionally liked to be talked to in such a manner. That intrigued Vish.

In the bedroom of the apartment next door, James Boston turned down the volume of a TV variety special and settled back with his ear near the wall vent.

As he listened, he watched a young female singer on the glowing screen soundlessly immerse herself so into her music that she cried.

From across Fifty-seventh Street, the bearded man scanned the face of the Beymer Building with his binoculars. He focused within minutes on window 29-12 and sat motionless but for the gentle rocking of his breathing.

27

Canby had found the location of the Holden farm by three that morning. He didn't share Strother's enthusiasm as to the likelihood of Vera Kivas panning out to be Jericho, but it was definitely a lead worth investigating. Since Strother had done the initial legwork on Dimitri and Vera Kivas, Canby sent Strother to the Holden farm.

The farm was off a seldom traveled alternate route about thirty miles beyond the New Jersey line. There was a side road, clearly marked with the Holdens' name lettered on a wooden sign nailed to an oak tree. Strother braked hard and made a sharp right turn onto the narrow dirt road.

Ahead he could see the roof of a small farmhouse beyond a grove of forked maple trees. There were a few cattle grazing in a field to the left, and to the right were rows of corn that appeared barren of husks.

When Strother drew nearer he saw that the farmhouse was a saltbox white frame structure with a wide front porch. Behind the house and off to the left was a leaning unpainted outbuilding with rotten wood doors hanging open to the sides like crippled wings. From the shadowed interior peered the spotlight-eyed gray nose of a tractor. A late-model Ford sedan was parked alongside the house, a trailer laden with feed sacks hitched to its rear bumper.

The dust raised by Strother's car caught up with him and briefly obscured his vision as he braked to a halt near the Ford.

As he stepped out of the air-conditioned car, the heat pressed down around him, instantly giving him a dull headache. The scream of crickets seemed uncommonly loud. He peeled off his sunglasses and squinted at the glare from the white house as he walked toward the porch.

A stocky man, shirtless, wearing stiff, new-looking bib overalls, opened the screen door and stepped out onto the porch as Strother approached. He had the grayish beginnings of a full beard, and thin, receding hair that was slightly curly and combed crosswise. He was steady-eyed and muscular.

"Yes, sir?" he said, somewhat gruffly, without smiling. Strother noticed a small coiled serpent tattooed on his left bicep.

"Are you Mr. Holden?"

"I am."

"David Strother's my name. I'd like to talk with your wife Nora about an important matter."

"Nora ain't here." Holden wiped a perspiring forearm across his sun-mottled face. His eyes were very pale and direct.

"Is she expected back soon?"

Holden stared at Strother as if debating within himself. "Fact is, Nora left me two weeks ago. Hasn't been back."

Strother shifted his weight in the hot sun. His shirt was plastered to his back. "Do you know where she went?"

"Nope." Holden gave a soft little laugh. "She don't want me to know where she's at. That's the idea of her leaving." He squinted up at the sun. "C'mon into the shade of the porch roof."

Strother accepted the invitation gladly. He stepped up on the uneven plank floor and said, "I wanted to talk to her about an old friend of hers, Vera Kivas."

Bracing a boot on the lowest porch rail, Holden spat into the dust. He scratched his gray-grizzled chin with a fingernail cracked and dirt-rimmed.

"Ain't seen nor thought of Vera for years," he said finally. "But sure, I remember her. When first we moved here she spent some time with us. Nora and her were close then, but I think they had some sort of falling out."

"Do you know where Vera is now?"

"No, sir."

"So that we know we're talking about the same woman, can you describe her?"

"Sure. Good-looking, slim, dark-haired. A smart little gal."

It was the second time Strother had heard Vera referred to as smart. "Smart in what way?"

"Not education-wise, necessarily. But shrewd. She had a way of looking at things and figuring them right off. Even being from the city, she picked up a lot about farming in the week she spent here. Picked it up faster than Nora did." Holden spat again into the dust, this time more vehemently. Clearly he hadn't forgiven Nora for straying.

Strother stood silently and watched a scraggly chicken peck at a deep rut left by a tractor tire.

"Vera was a little gal that was going to make her own way," Holden said. "But even a year after he died you wouldn't believe how she was still mooning over her husband. Maybe it was that religion her and Nora belonged to."

"Is your wife still a member of the Herras church?"

"No, she gave that up after we got married. Didn't seem to bother her none. She wasn't into religion that heavy."

"Was Vera Kivas?"

"Not as I know of." He smiled. "Vera had kind of a tendency to trouble the waters."

"How?"

"Don't know for sure, but I heard she was involved in a

154

few minor schemes in her old neighborhood. Nothing illegal, but still the kind of things that leave red faces and empty pockets."

"Was she ever caught at one of these schemes?"

"She was too smart to get caught. Besides, like I said, far as I know she always stayed legal. Most people don't even know about that side of her, but she confided in Nora. Vera had a way about her. Once a big department store made a mistake in their newspaper ad and Vera used it to trick them out of a hundred-dollar coat for half price. By the time they'd realized what happened, it was too late. Vera had her receipt and was wearing the coat."

"What did her husband think of that sort of thing?"

"Don't know. Never met him."

"I don't suppose you'd have an old photograph of your wife and Vera together."

Holden shook his head slowly, as if the sun were inhibiting his movements. "Got a few pictures of Nora, but that's all."

He went into the house, then returned in a few minutes with two snapshots of a heavy-featured blond woman with wide cheekbones and a resolute mouth.

"These are a few years old," he told Strother.

After gazing at the snapsots, Strother thanked him. He gave Holden his phone number scribbled on a piece of paper and asked him to have Nora call if she returned.

"I guess this heat is tough on livestock," he remarked, stepping down from the porch into the fierceness of the sun.

"Not so tough since Vera visited," Holden said.

Strother stepped back onto the porch. "What has Vera Kivas got to do with that?"

Holden appeared a bit surprised. "That week she came to stay here, it was for a reason. She helped Nora and me open up the creek into an irrigation ditch that runs along that hill."

"Helped in what way?"

"With dynamite. Otherwise I'd have had to hire a bulldozer and spend a fortune. But Vera knew how to use dynamite to change the course of the creek. Her husband was

155

some sort of demolition expert. Used to blow up big buildings. Guess Vera picked up what she knew from him."

Holden was surprised to see Strother smile, wave a hasty good-bye and almost run to his car.

28

"We can't find Vera Kivas," Canby said.

Strother paced the scuff-marked floor of Canby's office. "But we have to find her—she's it, I'm sure!"

Canby rotated gently in his swivel chair and observed Strother. Up to this point, the young architect had performed admirably and in restrained fashion. Now he was excited, which was to be expected from a nonprofessional. Though he didn't know it, this was when he was most apt to make a mistake.

"The fact that no one in her old neighborhood knows her whereabouts doesn't necessarily mean she deliberately went undercover," Canby said. "A lot of people, for a variety of reasons, break clean with their pasts."

"Not as clean as Vera Kivas broke, without leaving even a photograph behind so we might know what she looked like."

"Possibly she left the area, then returned. The explosives supposedly have been in place for years. My guess is that if

157

she is who we want, we'll find out it was Dimitri Kivas who actually planted them."

Strother paused in his pacing, then sat down. He hadn't thought of that possibility. But what did it matter now? Dimitri Kivas was dead, and his widow knew enough about his unique trade to kill thousands if she chose to do so. If the million dollars wasn't paid sometime day after tomorrow.

"We're still covering everything," Canby assured him. "Interviewing neighborhood people, checking cross-directories, auto license records, welfare rolls, hospital records. The FBI has already informed us that Vera Kivas has no prints in their master file."

"Which means she's never been arrested or in the service," Strother said despondently.

"Which is something," Canby said. "The most trivial bits of information have a way of suddenly fitting together and taking on unexpected importance, like a kaleidoscope image that all at once forms a recognizable picture."

"But isn't there anything else we can do right now?" Strother slapped the arm of his chair in exasperation.

"It's all being done. Have patience; reserve yourself for when you might be needed." Even as he gave the advice, Canby knew how difficult it was to follow. That was the unconvincing side of most advice.

Strother let out a loud, trailing sigh. "You're right." He smiled in vague embarrassment. "I guess I've been acting like the amateur I am."

"All in all," Canby said, "you're doing well." He was relieved to see Strother gain control of himself. "Since we seem to have hit on a natural lull in the investigation, why don't we have an early lunch?"

"I'm supposed to meet Ann for lunch at noon."

"Give her a call," Canby said, motioning with his head toward his desk phone. "See if she can make it a little early. I'll ask Molly if she wants to go. We can eat at Durell's ahead of the lunchtime crowd." He wanted to inject some measure

158

of normality into Strother's life so the architect could maintain his perspective. Canby knew from his own past how important that could be.

Strother considered the suggestion for a moment, then agreed. He phoned Ann at the ad agency, where she was discussing layouts for a new campaign, and she told him she could be free in fifteen minutes. She would meet them at Durell's at eleven-thirty.

Durell's was becoming crowded despite the early hour. When Canby entered with Strother and Molly, Ann Ferris was already there, seated with elegant perfect posture on the small wooden bench just inside the doorway. She had already reserved a table.

Maury the maître d' led them like trusting mice through the maze of angled mahogany partitions to a reasonably private table near the rear of the restaurant. They sat and ordered drinks, and Canby could see Molly sizing up Ann Ferris's simple but chic tan dress and patterned neck scarf. He wanted to assure Molly that she didn't have a thing to envy in Ann and decided that later he would do just that. Undoubtedly, of the two women Ann was the more beautiful in the classical sense, but she wasn't more beautiful to Canby. He mused as he often had that beauty and ugliness, truth and falsehood, were at the same time simple and complicated.

As Canby sipped his manhattan, he saw with satisfaction that Ann's presence exercised a soothing effect on Strother.

The four of them talked of personal, inconsequential matters, but always the Morgell Trust Building case was there with them. They didn't speak of it simply because none of them had anything new to say.

Everyone at the table except Canby had the steak special with Burgundy wine. Canby wasn't that hungry and ordered only a chef's salad and coffee.

It was when they were almost finished eating, when Ann was telling them about various photographic techniques, that

Strother abruptly lowered a bit of steak he'd been about to consume. His fork made a tiny clinking sound on the china plate.

"Yes," he said softly. "Yes, of course!"

"I'm glad you understand the various aspects of wide-angle photography," Ann told him, unperturbed by his interruption.

"It was in that batch of literature Jamess handed me at the church," Strother went on. He wiped his lips with his napkin and looked across the table at Canby. "When I was reading about the history and doctrine of the Herras religion, I came across a piece of information that didn't register at the time as important. As in a lot of other religions, one of the Herras customs is to bury a few choice representative objects with the deceased."

"This doesn't strike me as proper dinner conversation," Ann told him.

"She's right," Molly said, as if Ann were serious.

Strother ignored them. "Among the items the Herrases often are buried with are likenesses of their survivors to whom they were closest in life."

"And you think we might find a photograph of Vera Kivas in her husband's casket?" Canby asked.

"Of course we might!"

"That's going a bit far," Ann said.

"The idea's grotesque," Molly agreed. "And besides that, impractical. By this time, if there was a likeness of the man's wife in his casket, it would be ruined by rot and mildew. The photo's subject would be unrecognizable."

"That depends on whether or not Kivas was buried in a sealed casket!" Strother said, unconsciously reaching across the table and clutching Molly's elbow with unnecessary strength.

Canby watched Strother realize what he'd done and quickly withdraw his hand.

"It's worth a chance," Strother said in a subdued but still vibrant voice.

Molly nudged away her plate as if her appetite had been

affected. "If you ask me, the idea seems ghoulish. Desperate and ghoulish."

"I've got to make a phone call," Strother said. He dropped his folded napkin onto the table, stood and walked toward the foyer, where the public phone was located.

Canby knew what number he was going to dial.

"Really, Dex," Molly said, "don't you think this is going overboard? What will the newspapers say about it?"

"I don't know," Canby answered to both questions, finishing his salad. "Maybe it's all academic anyway."

But when Strother returned to the table his lean face was taut with the excitement that glinted in his eyes. The hunter had found the spoor once more.

"I talked to Jamess at the Herras church," he said, sitting back down. "He isn't sure, but he thinks a small photograph of Mrs. Kivas was among the items buried with her husband —in a sealed coffin."

"He isn't sure," Molly said.

"I think you ought to forget this," Ann said to Strother.

"We can't forget it," Canby spoke up. "Where is Kivas buried?"

"In Faith Assumption Cemetery in Queens." Strother gulped down the remainder of his glass of wine. A tiny amber droplet, like diluted blood, clung to the side of his chin as if he were an improbable, bespectacled Dracula. Then it dropped and stained his shirt.

Canby stood up. "You three have dessert," he said. "I'll tell Maury to put this on my tab."

"Where are you going?" Strother asked.

"To seek a court order for the exhumation of the body of Dimitri Kivas."

They watched him thread his way through the crowded restaurant toward the door, a burdened, somewhat stoop-shouldered man moving with quiet, desperate purpose. He spoke briefly to Maury without glancing back at them and went out.

"This has been a hell of a lunch," Ann said.

29

1976

With a damp paper towel, she dabbed at the stain on the front of her slightly threadbare dress. Something greasy. Removing it without a trace was impossible. She decided that she simply wouldn't take off her coat. Dropping the wadded paper towel into the wastebasket, she walked toward the door to the living room.

"Time for the doctor," she said to her husband.

He got up from where he'd been sitting before the TV, watching election returns. She was struck by how much thinner he seemed to have become even since yesterday. It was the clothes, she told herself, his dark slacks and the blue shirt that had always been too large for him.

"Carter is what they want," he observed, walking to the TV and switching it off. "Maybe he'll do something about the inflation that's going to make this routine checkup cost us seventy-five dollars."

"Maybe."

"No," he decided, putting on his coat, "he won't. I know he won't."

She was pleased to see that he looked his stocky, powerful self in the bulky overcoat. And she'd be relieved to find out why he'd lost so much weight in the past few months. She hoped she would be relieved. "The money shouldn't matter to us now," she said.

"You're right," he told her. He smiled at the thought. "We're ready now to carry out the last part of the plan. Soon the preparation pays."

"Preparation always does."

"Not always," he said, "but it can be an adequate substitute for luck."

She put on her coat and opened the apartment door for him. "I'll drive you," she said.

"You don't have to."

"I didn't say I had to." They stared at each other. She'd irritated him, but right now she didn't care. She stepped close to him and kissed him on the lips, surprising him.

"You'll catch what I've got," he warned with a brief smile.

"I want that."

He touched her shoulder gently, with an odd indecision—unlike him—and they left.

Cancer.

Directly, with seeming lack of emotion, he had told her he had cancer.

The second day in the hospital he had told her that, making the room rock, whirl, then steady, like a mad carnival ride winding down. The cancer was in his pancreas, he said. There was no way to predict exactly how long it would take to kill him.

She wanted him to decide not to die; she felt that if he decided to defy Death, Death would bend to him.

But he was an intelligent as well as a willful man. He knew. Sometimes the universe crushes. He accepted.

163

They let him return home to die slowly, away from cool tile, passing footsteps in the hall and the scent of disinfectant.

"I want you to continue with the plan," he told her on the first night back in their flat. He always referred to it simply as "the plan," as if it were some natural underlying design that had always existed.

"I don't know how," she replied. "I don't want to."

"You'll learn. You'll want to. The difficult part is finished, the years of laying the groundwork. I'll teach you what you need to know."

She knew what was going on in his mind. This way, even in death, he would triumph. For her. For him. She wouldn't deny him, never could and never wanted to.

"All right," she said.

He kissed her. She cried for the first time in years, vaguely surprised that the tears were uncontrollable.

She actually realized then in the core of her that he was dying.

30

The Present

Canby obtained the court order as quickly as possible. Still, it was ten that evening before Canby, Strother and an assistant M.E. named Caruthers stood near the center of the flat green surface that was Faith Assumption Cemetery in Queens, and watched while two city workmen dug. The scene was illuminated by portable radiant lanterns, and beyond the bright circle of light were shadows of unreality.

It was obvious that someone had been here before them. The Kivas grave had been disturbed and was only half filled with dirt. It appeared as if whoever had tampered with the grave was frightened away before the coffin was reached.

Canby had the workmen use the cemetery's mechanical gravedigger to remove most of the earth, until there was danger of damaging the coffin or its contents. Now the work required shovels.

Most of the graves in the cemetery were marked in the same manner as Dimitri Kivas's, with ground-level brass plaques bearing simple inscriptions. There were a few dozen headstones jutting here and there on the flat landscape, like moonlit sentinels keeping watch on the strikingly ordinary traffic rushing past on Fulton Avenue just beyond the spiked iron fence. The cemetery reminded Canby of a morbid painting he'd created in his youth.

As the shovels thunked into soft earth, and dirt meant never to be disturbed sprayed up intermittently from the open grave, Canby stood staring at the inscription on Kivas's brass plaque. Below the dead man's birth and death dates, the plaque read simply, "He is free." But even in death, Dimitri Kivas wasn't entirely free. Rather, his remains weren't.

Now the shovels were regularly striking something more firm than earth. Canby had witnessed exhumations before, but something within him seemed to draw up with each crisp, faintly hollow sound from below. He glanced over at Strother and saw that the lanky architect was feeling the same effects. Strother's narrow face contorted slightly with each shovel blow.

The assistant M.E. seemed unaffected. He was the only one not perspiring, a short blond man wearing a pale blue shirt with the sleeves rolled up. "Almost there," he observed absently.

Canby grunted, watching the swishing flashes of passing headlights beyond the cemetery fence. "Let's hope somebody without a court order hasn't been there before us."

Within fifteen minutes the cemetery hoist was straining to raise its burden.

The coffin broke ground slowly, like some subterranean behemoth unaccustomed to the light. It was scrolled, obviously expensive, sealed with thumbscrews. Some undertaker had done a slick selling job. With a loud moaning and squealing of pulleys and cables, the ponderous coffin was eased to the side of the open grave and allowed to settle on the ground.

There was a brief wait until the fingerprint crew arrived.

The outside of the casket yielded mostly smears. If anyone had opened it recently, they'd worn gloves. The results of the fingerprint tests were what Canby had expected.

All of the thumbscrews that sealed the lid were still firmly secured; they might well have been undisturbed for years. With difficulty and a few well-timed curses, the two workmen loosened them. Canby nodded and the lid was raised to release the faint, acrid odor of time.

It was impossible not to look at the ghastly, determined face in the coffin. In the shadowed light it appeared sunken, eyes closed, lips drawn tight. Despite the work of a skilled embalmer, Dimitri Kivas looked as though one touch would shatter his delicate, crystalline lifelessness to dust. Canby willed his eyes away from the face and saw several objects on either side of the body in the casket.

One of the objects was a small, gold-framed photograph of a woman.

"You were right," Canby said to Strother. He gingerly picked up the photograph by its frame, careful not to touch the obscenely neat dark suit in which Kivas's corpse was clothed. Even in the faint light he could see that the photograph was relatively undamaged by its years underground.

From where he'd moved to, several feet from the open casket, Strother stepped jerkily forward and peered over Canby's shoulder at the photograph. Better light was needed to plainly discern Vera Kivas's features.

"You can keep it," the assistant M.E. said, motioning with a pale hand toward the framed photograph.

Canby nodded. He'd already known there was no need to replace the photograph in the casket. It was far too important for that. Or he hoped it was.

"Close it and put him back," he said, pointing to the open casket. He tasted the bitterness of bile.

"There's a reporter I know," Caruthers, the assistant M.E., said, watching as the coffin lid was closed. It was his job to stay here until Kivas was properly reburied. "We've got sort of an arrangement and I'd like to phone him about this. I won't if you say not to."

"I say not to. If this photograph hits the papers and TV, or even news of it does, whoever we're searching for will go so far underground we'll need that mechanical digger to get them out. Maybe now, for the first time, we'll know who we're going to all this trouble to find. You fuck it up by calling in the media and you'll be the one who's hard to find."

Caruthers appeared surprised, more hurt than angry. A large moth attracted by the light flitted against his face. He brushed it away violently. "Well, that's why I brought it up. To clear it with you or have it nixed. But the media will get onto it soon enough anyway."

"But no sooner than they have to. Not by way of you."

"Not by way of me. You can depend on that, Captain."

Canby was furious that Caruthers would even consider impeding the investigation by phoning the press. Then, through his anger, it occurred to him that Molly might be right about his pushing too hard. Caruthers *had* in effect asked permission. Canby considered apologizing to Caruthers, then decided that if he didn't, the assistant M.E. would be less likely to talk if he were directly approached by any member of the media. Better to let the matter stand.

The hoist began to squeal and moan again as the coffin was lowered back into the grave. The sound depressed and unnerved Canby. He nodded to Strother, who looked slightly ill in the pale moonlight, and the two men left Caruthers standing by the still-open grave and walked toward the cemetery gate.

The ground was soft beneath Canby's shoes, oddly reminiscent of flesh. In a cemetery like this, with all ground-level markers for easy mowing, it was difficult to know if you were walking on a grave. He was glad when they set foot on the blacktop drive that curved in from the iron gate with its flanking stone columns.

At the gate, Strother paused and glanced back. "That's the most persuasive argument for cremation I've ever seen."

Canby didn't answer as they walked on, the small gold-framed photograph heavy in his suitcoat pocket. Despite the obvious justification for his act, he couldn't help feeling somewhat like a grave robber.

Outside the cemetery gate, Molly and Ann were waiting in Canby's unmarked car. Canby and Strother got into the front seat, and Canby reached to the dashboard and turned on the car's interior dome light. Everything became sharp yet somehow colorless.

"Did you find anything?" Molly asked.

Canby nodded wordlessly.

"I suppose it would be tactless to say you two look as if you've seen a ghost," Ann said.

Canby removed the photograph from his pocket and held it up so they could examine it beneath the light.

Within the delicate gold frame was the likeness of an attractive, dark-haired woman. She had fine-boned, slightly haughty features dominated by heavy-lidded, almost reptilian eyes. Hypnotic eyes.

"There are possibilities in those eyes," Ann commented, perfectly serious.

"Any man would think so," Molly said, misunderstanding. She had seen too many "noncriminal" physical types booked for crimes that staggered the imagination for her to connect appearance with criminal potential.

"Let's hope we're onto something," Canby said, switching off the interior light and starting the car. "Something real."

They pulled away from the curb and picked up speed quickly, moving parallel to the high spiked iron fence that separated them from the land of the dead.

Canby was busy through most of the rest of that night. The only sleep he obtained was in small periods at his desk, between bursts of activity and phone calls seemingly spaced to keep him from dozing more than fifteen minutes in succession. Time, he mused sleepily, over his sixth cup of coffee that night, becomes eventually the major factor in everyone's life. Time is the only true enemy, and sooner or later it will show itself and mock your inability to cope with it.

Norris buzzed him just then to report an incoming call Canby had been expecting. Canby breathed in deeply to drive

169

away his morbidity and come fully awake. Then he poured another cup of black coffee and picked up the phone. Through his nerve-edged drowsiness, he realized somewhat proudly that he was accomplishing a great deal that night.

By the next morning, copies of the Kivas photograph had been circulated around the Police Department with strict instructions to keep their existence confidential as far as the news media were concerned.

But only the news media.

Every man on the department had orders to show the photograph on his beat, and to report any response that might constitute even the thinnest lead. The media would learn of the mass inquiry soon enough to include it in the evening editions of both printed and televised news. But by that time Canby hoped to have some results. If information about the photograph inquiry was withheld long enough, it might enable the police to close on the suspect while she still had no idea that her appearance was a factor in the search for her.

More and more, Canby was becoming convinced that Vera Kivas was the key. She had to be.

A clear sky foretold another sweltering day, adding to Canby's agony as he awaited pertinent information and hoped the story wouldn't hit the news too soon.

He didn't go home. He changed clothes at the precinct house, then sat at his desk to work. By seven-thirty he was asleep, his head cradled in his arms on the cluttered desk top.

Norris, himself as weary as he'd ever been, spotted Canby through the partly opened door and kept everyone, including Molly, out of the office. As he had so many times during the past thirty-one years, Norris reflected that being a cop was a one-of-a-kind occupation.

31

Will Kerr, the precinct cop assigned to a section of blocks north of East Fifty-sixth Street, wasn't used to walking a beat. He'd spent his past five years on the force in a two-man patrol car, cruising the area's teeming, often elegant avenues. It took a certain type of cop to handle some of the wealthy inhabitants of the district. Kerr had that knack; that's why he'd been assigned his duties and left alone. Left alone until now.

Today there would be no riding in the patrol car with his partner. Today it was special duty for almost everyone in the department. Kerr had been given his copy of the woman's photo, as had everyone else at muster this morning. No one had been told specifically who the woman was, or why they had to trace her, but each man had instructions to show the photo to as many people on his beat as possbile on the off chance there'd be an identification. They were not to talk about the photo, which was an easy order to follow.

The object was to flash the woman's picture around without arousing the news media, Kerr was sure. But that didn't make sense. If the department wanted her identified fast, the way to do it would be to plaster her picture in the newspapers and on TV. Or maybe the department higher-ups wanted to find her before she knew they were looking. Now that made sense. Except that Kerr was sure the higher-ups didn't have that much guile.

The day didn't figure to be enjoyable. And to make things even more aggravating, the temperature already had climbed well into the uncomfortable range. If he had a nice, high-paying job in one of these big air-conditioned office buildings, he wouldn't have to suffer in the heat. But getting that sort of job took connections, and Kerr's choice of parents had been unfortunate. The rich got richer and the poor got hotter. And tireder.

Kerr's feet hurt as he trudged across Fifty-seventh, then stood waiting for the light to change. He was twenty pounds heavier than when he'd last walked a beat, and he felt every ounce pressing down on the soles of his shoes. A big man, shamelessly gone to fat, he had a long, jowly face and basset-sad eyes. A rich bitch carrying a Lord & Taylor paper bag jostled him for position on the curb. He wished to hell he could sit down.

When Kerr had crossed the street he saw the entrance to the Beymer Building and remembered the coffee shop off the lobby. He decided that would be a good place to show the photo around, and he could have a cup of coffee and sit for a while. It was only eight o'clock. He regretted having eaten breakfast so early at home, but maybe he could force down a roll with his coffee.

The coffee shop was crowded with people eating breakfast before they had to hurry on to their jobs. Kerr saw an empty stool at the counter and squeezed between two businessmen types studying their newspapers. He sighed deeply as he sat down, and both men glanced up from their reading, then ignored him completely.

Myra the counter waitress came over and took his order. She looked the same as always this morning, Kerr noted, wondering why she didn't wear her hair differently and have that mole on the bridge of her nose removed. He sat listening idly to the buzz of voices and the clinking of china and silverware.

When Myra returned with his cup of coffee and a cherry danish, he showed her the photo and asked if she knew who the woman was. Myra was glad for a chance to stand still. Management wouldn't bother her if she was talking to the law.

"I never seen her," she said. "She's a beauty, though. Like in show business. I'd remember her."

"She's not that much of a beauty," Kerr said, following instructions. "Imagine her wearing something plain, with her hair mussed up or cut different."

Myra shook her head. "She ain't familiar. Unless she gained fifty pounds and had plastic surgery, I never seen her."

Kerr watched Myra drift back down the counter toward a newly arrived customer, a shabby, intense-looking man with a full beard. Then he concentrated on his roll and coffee.

He showed the photo around to some of the other customers at the counter before leaving, so he could honestly say he'd done his duty.

32

1977

He was dead. She returned to the flat and stood staring at the tangible silence, the quiet, inanimate walls, the immobile furniture, the corner of the bed visible through the open bedroom doorway. There was nothing now alive in the flat other than herself, no indefinable stirring in the next room, no object moved by a hand other than her own, no reason to think about anyone other than herself.

But no, that wasn't quite true. She had reason to think often of her husband, and of what his life had meant. Would mean.

She was beginning to understand. Maybe we were nothing if not our dreams. And like the pain of our sins, our dreams could be bequeathed and survive the death of the body.

If only someone had the will to keep them alive.

A week after her husband's funeral, she received the hospital and doctor bills. They amounted to over seventy-five hundred dollars. The cancer had won its macabre race with the insurance company, thrived well beyond the expiration date of the policy's hospital cost coverage. She stared at the bills for a long time, and then she laughed. She could imagine her husband laughing with her. He was the only man she'd known whose laughter conveyed determination.

Well, she was determined now. She might need help, but she knew where she could find it. Probably her husband had understood that.

Three days later she moved from the four rooms that had been their home, leaving no forwarding address, telling no one of her plans.

33

The Present

By eleven o'clock that morning, they knew where she was.

She walked into the seventeenth precinct house, trailing a long, fringed cape lined with green satin. She was flanked by a meek-looking man wearing an obvious toupee and by a bulky, self-important type in an expensive gray vested suit that almost perfectly matched his eyes and hair. She was mad as hell.

"I want to see Captain Dexter P. Canby," she told Norris, staring a slow-burning hole through him with those now familiar hooded eyes. She was heavier than in her photograph, older. The added weight and years gave her a certain air of authority that for a moment threw even Norris.

And he'd like to see you, he almost told her, squinting down at her to make doubly sure he was looking at Vera Kivas.

Norris asked her to wait please and buzzed Canby's office.

"Vera Kivas is out here and wants to see you, Captain,"

came Norris's calm voice over the intercom.

In an equally calm voice, only slightly betraying his disbelief, Canby told Norris to send Mrs. Kivas in.

Canby opened the blinds behind him, above the air conditioner, so the light would be at his back, and sat waiting. The air conditioner began its squealing, and he slapped it almost absently and it resumed its smooth hum.

"Mrs. Kivas," he said, standing when she entered still accompanied by her two companions. A high-voltage jolt of recognition struck him. He was looking at features he had first gazed upon beside a moldering corpse.

"I'm told you're responsible for having my photograph shown all over town," she said, standing with her weight evenly distributed on both feet, lending her an angry gracelessness.

"Easy, Gwen," the man in the vested suit told her softly, and Canby felt a hollow apprehension in his stomach.

"I'm responsible," he told her. "Who are these two?"

"My attorney, Martin Guilcrest, and my manager, Barry Duke." Duke was the smaller of the two, with a slightly crooked toupee and an indecisive mouth and chin. He stared at Canby as if frightened of him.

Guilcrest, the one in the tailored gray suit, stood with a studied calm and total lack of movement.

"Why don't you all sit down?" Canby invited, motioning toward the office's uncomfortable wood chairs. No one sat.

"Ms. Cardee deserves an explanation," Guilcrest said. He had a smooth courtroom voice.

"Ms. Cardee?"

Guilcrest nodded slowly yet firmly, like a man holding aces and calling a bet. "Ms. Gwen Cardee. Possibly you've heard of her."

"I've heard of her as Vera Kivas," Canby said.

"Who the hell is Vera Kivas?" the woman asked.

Duke cleared his throat as if to speak, but Guilcrest shot him a superior, cautioning glance.

"Vera Kivas is the widow of a man named Dimitri Kivas.

We think she has something to do with the Morgell Trust Building destruction."

Gwen Cardee glared at Canby. Guilcrest's gray eyes took on a surprised, wary look at the mention of the Morgell Trust Building. The game had changed in a way not immediately comprehensible.

Canby decided he'd had enough of being the recipient of their anger.

"How did you discover your photo was being shown?" he asked.

"I think," Guilcrest said, "that you should do no more talking here today, Gwen."

Canby stared at him, at all three of them. "Then I'll do some talking." He sat down, leaned back and rocked slightly in his chair. "We want Vera Kivas. She seems to have disappeared, leaving not so much as her photograph behind. A photograph of this woman"—he pointed at Gwen Cardee—"was removed last night from Dimitri Kivas's grave, reproduced and distributed among the department's officers to show the public. Now, I'm going to repeat my question. How did you discover the photo was being shown?" He looked directly at Gwen Cardee.

"My client can walk out of here, Captain," Guilcrest said. "You can't compel her to answer these questions unless she's being charged."

"She won't walk out. I'll charge her if necessary."

Guilcrest assessed Canby carefully, his shrewd eyes narrowed and somewhat puzzled. "You'll charge her with what?"

"The murder of nine hundred and eleven people and the destruction of the Morgell Trust Building."

"But you're wrong, and you know it."

"There's a possibility I might be right."

Guilcrest sat down in the nearest chair and leaned forward. "Speaking candidly, Captain, if you charge Ms. Cardee we both know your ass will be in a sling. It might hasten the end of your career."

Canby sat silently.

"Talk to the man, Gwen," Duke said evenly, assuming a firm command incongruous with his appearance. Guilcrest didn't argue.

"I saw my photo on a TV news bulletin at ten this morning," Gwen Cardee said. She seemed less angry and slightly confused. "The newscaster said that all the city cops were showing it to people, trying to locate me."

"Now that we've found you," Canby said, "if you're not Vera Kivas, who are you? Who is Gwen Cardee?"

She seemed momentarily insulted. "I'm a fashion model. Not the most famous now, but a few years ago I was on the cover of almost any magazine you'd pick up."

"Ten years ago," Duke said. She glowered at him with her potent eyes but he moved closer to her and patted her shoulder.

"Do you remember that particular photograph?" Canby asked.

"Of course. For a while it was the one I sent to everyone who wrote to me. It was my 'official' photo; I autographed them and mailed them or handed them out by the thousands."

"That's no exaggeration," Duke said to Canby.

"Have you ever heard of Dimitri or Vera Kivas?" Canby asked Gwen Cardee.

She shrugged graceful shoulders beneath her cape. "Of course not."

"Any idea how your photograph could have gotten into Dimitri Kivas's coffin?"

"God, no!" She suddenly giggled, destroying her attitude of sophistication. "I mean, nobody's *that* big a fan."

"You might be surprised," Canby said. But he knew how the photo had gotten into the Kivas grave. Whoever had disturbed the grave *had* reached the casket before the police, and had replaced the Vera Kivas photo with one of Gwen Cardee. The attractive model did fit Vera Kivas's general description, except that Gwen Cardee was much taller. The autograph on the photo had been cropped before the substitution was made in what was no doubt the original gold frame. The obviously

179

aged condition of the frame had helped to fool Canby.

"Do you admit this is all a mistake, Captain?" Guilcrest asked.

Canby ignored him, refusing to aid him in laying the groundwork for any future legal action.

"Where do you live, Ms. Cardee?"

She gave an address in a good area of midtown Manhattan, an apartment building that catered to people connected with entertainment or the arts.

"Are you a working model now?"

She appeared faintly embarrassed, as if he'd suggested she wasn't a real model at all. He realized he might have phrased the question more tactfully.

"For Kitty-clean," she said.

"Kitty-clean?"

"The cat litter. I'm going to appear in their fall advertising campaign."

A long way down from being a top fashion model, Canby thought. For a second he felt sorry for Gwen Cardee. Then he remembered her address. She must have made a great deal of money when she was at the top of her profession.

"Do you have any identification on you?" he asked.

She reached into the oversized purse she was carrying and handed him her driver's license, some well-preserved fashion magazine covers from the late sixties, and a photo identical to the one that had been slipped into the gold frame in Dimitri Kivas's coffin. The glamour shots on the magazine covers were of a younger, more vital Gwen Cardee. This photo was uncropped, and autographed by her beneath the unimaginative inscription "All the best."

"You're welcome to keep that," she said.

Canby thanked her and after examining the license and magazine covers handed them back to her. He laid the photograph carefully on his desk.

"I don't want to detain you, Ms. Cardee, but I am going to ask you to stay in town."

"I want to cooperate, Captain."

180

Canby wasn't sure if she was sincere or merely thinking of the great deal of publicity that might open doors for her that had long been closed.

"Is she free to go?" Guilcrest asked.

Canby smiled. "She was always free to go."

"Captain," Gwen Cardee said, "I want you to know I'm sorry about being angry. I mean, I didn't know what it was about."

"Everybody is familiar with your face again," Canby said. "Maybe you can turn what happened into something positive." He wanted to apologize to her but thought better of it in front of Guilcrest.

"I think we can do just that," Duke said. He shook hands with Canby before the three of them left the office.

Canby immediately picked up the phone and punched a button.

"Follow the woman just leaving," he said briskly. "Name Gwendolyne Cardwell, a.k.a. Gwen Cardee, age thirty-seven, tall, medium complexion, green eyes. Accompanied by two men. She lives at 153 West Fifty-eighth Street, apartment 67E, works as a model—a genuine model. Let me know where and when she sets down and put a watch on her apartment."

He punched another button and gave instructions to relay orders to cease inquiring about the Kivas grave photo.

When Canby replaced the receiver the hollowness in his stomach became a painful gnawing sensation. He knew he should have double-checked, shown the casket photo to someone who'd known Vera Kivas. That he hadn't done this was inexcusable, despite the fact that the photo fit the Kivas woman's description and had been removed from her husband's coffin. The grave had been deliberately left to appear as if whoever had disturbed it hadn't reached the coffin. And the fact that a photograph *was* there when the coffin was opened seemed to confirm that whoever had been digging in the grave hadn't completed their task.

A siren sounded faintly outside, and down the hall a teletype machine clattered briefly as if in alarm as a door was opened, then closed. The thing that was gnawing in Canby's stomach grew more ferocious.

There was little doubt in his mind that Gwen Cardee was genuine.

He picked up the receiver again, noticing that it was still moist and warm from his grip during the previous call.

He knew he had to phone the mayor.

34

"She'll probably sue us," Mayor Danner said when Canby had told him on the phone about the Vera Kivas fiasco and the visit by Gwen Cardee. The mayor didn't seem particularly excited about the prospect; it was the least of his troubles.

"I've received further instructions from Jericho," he told Canby, brushing aside the Gwen Cardee matter. "I've already sent a tape of the telephone conversation to you by messenger, just a few minutes ago, but I'll tell you what was said."

"Was it the same voice?" Canby asked.

"As far as I could tell. I figured your men in the police lab could say for sure."

"I hope so. What were the instructions?"

"The money is to be packed in a brown American Tourister suitcase, model number 54X233, and held at my sister's home until further word. Sometime before noon tomorrow there will be further instructions by phone, to be received at Muriel's, my sister's, apartment."

"So he still expects the money to be held under guard,"

Canby said, "or he'd have insisted on another method of delivery."

"Why shouldn't he want it under guard?" Danner asked. "At this point he probably regards it as his own money but for a few formalities."

"But dangerous formalities. Did he say anything else?"

"No, only the instructions, almost word for word as I've related them to you. He was terse, to the point."

"Did he sound nervous?"

"There was no way to tell, the way his voice was distorted." Danner paused. "Maybe you should know, I'm starting to get pressure from the governor. Publicly he's placed this thing in my hands, but privately I think he wants me not to pay."

"Has he said so?"

"No, it isn't done that way, Captain Canby. It's done by implication, with an eye to the record and how it will look if certain events do or don't occur. He doesn't know precisely which side of the fence to jump to because he isn't sure how this is all going to end. So he takes opposite stands, public and private. That way he can point to either set of statements and actions, depending on the outcome of our dilemma. But if everything goes smoothly, the public will never hear of our private conversations and his implication that we should take a tough stand."

Canby rapped softly with disgust on his desk. He felt like saying a few things about politics as an occupation, but he reminded himself of who was on the other end of the line.

"Somebody's getting to our great and good governor," Danner said with thoughtful irony, "exerting the same sort of pressure on him that he's exerting on me."

"It shouldn't be difficult to figure out who can put pressure on a governor."

"Oh, it doesn't necessarily have to be pressure from above, Captain. He might be influenced by the persuasive powers of someone we never heard of, someone circumstances have given cards to play for this particular hand."

Canby thought back to his conversation with Carl Gaines.

Maybe he should tell Danner about that. But what had Gaines actually said that if repeated would evoke Danner's mistrust of his chief aide? Implication again. Politics. Canby decided to keep silent for now about Gaines.

"I can have the money at my sister's apartment on East Eighty-seventh Street anytime you want it there," Danner said. "I've already sent out for the requested suitcase model. It's not a large suitcase, according to the clerk at the store. About like a two-suiter. Will all that money fit in a suitcase that size?"

"It will fit," Canby said. "You'd be surprised how flat money can be packed. I'll detail two men to pick it up and deliver it to your sister's address, where it will be guarded."

"Muriel won't be in any danger, will she?"

"She doesn't even have to be there," Canby said. "Why don't you suggest to her that she visit a friend or relative while we make use of her apartment?"

"I've already done that," Danner said. "But I wanted to make sure it was all right before she left. She's willing to stay."

"My advice is that she leave."

"I'll tell her. I'll make her leave!"

"Is noon all right for the pickup?" Canby asked.

"Noon at my office."

"This might sound silly, Mayor Danner, but be sure to ask my men for identification. They'll be expecting that."

"Of course."

"Another thing," Canby said. "Don't be too discouraged about this Gwen Cardee incident."

"You mean about a possible lawsuit?"

"Not that." Canby was sure Gwen Cardee wouldn't sue, but he didn't consider the opinion worth mentioning. "What I mean is that we learned something valuable from it. If someone went to the trouble to replace Vera Kivas's photo in that casket, Vera Kivas is involved in the Morgell Trust bombing. We can be sure of that now."

"Involved," Danner said, "but harder to locate in time."

185

"Not necessarily," Canby said. "Only about a dozen people, including the judge who issued the court order for an exhumation, knew what was going to happen at the cemetery and when."

The sound in Canby's receiver was Mayor Danner actually chuckling. "God, I hadn't thought of that! It narrows it down!"

"By several million. Replacing that photograph was a desperation move."

"What do you plan on doing now, questioning the people who knew ahead of time about the exhumation?"

"I've got another idea. But let me think about it some more."

"Don't think about it much longer," Danner said. "The hands on my clocks seem to be moving faster."

When Danner had hung up, Canby composed a list of the people who'd known about the exhumation. There were the original three besides Canby who'd formulated the idea in Durell's Restaurant, Judge Hanniman, who'd issued the court order for exhumation, the M.E. and his assistant Caruthers, Hanniman's secretary, Verna Kruger, the clerks at the courthouse who'd recorded the court order, and several of Faith Assumption Cemetery's personnel. The two city workmen who'd done the digging hadn't known of their exact assignment far enough ahead of time to have tampered with the grave before the legal exhumation.

Canby had Mathews come into his office. The lieutenant stood looking even more misproportioned and disheveled than usual. He'd been working hard on matters Canby had been ignoring.

"I want the most reliable men available to get on this immediately," Canby told him. He handed Mathews the list of names. "Have a photograph obtained for every name on that list, and have it done secretly if possible. I need the photos on my desk within hours."

"They'll be there," Mathews said. He hitched his belt to shift his ill-fitting uniform pants. "I can get you the municipal employees' photos from their files within half an hour."

"Do it," Canby said, "but take forty-five minutes and get ten copies of each."

As he watched Mathews hurry out to issue orders, Canby was strangely relaxed. There was nothing he could do for the next hour. And at last he really sensed that he was making progress. Something was stirring in the murky depths of his mind, where the predators swam.

If he didn't know "where," he knew "who."

35

When the photographs were assembled, Canby assigned a
squad to comb the neighborhood where the Kivases had
lived, showing the photos to anyone who might have known
Vera or Dimitri Kivas. He hoped that one of the twelve reproduced photographs would be of someone who'd had contact
with the Kivases or was at least known in the neighborhood.

Canby phoned Strother to let him know what was happening, and to assure Strother that something positive had come
out of his idea to exhume Dimitri Kivas. Strother seemed
pleased on the surface though still deeply despondent. He
asked if he could help, and Canby told him to stay near
his phone or leave a number where he might be reached.

Then Canby sat and watched two air-conditioning repairmen work on the intermittently squealing window unit behind his desk. If he'd requested the repairmen, he couldn't
remember. Norris must have called them.

They were in the office less than twenty minutes before declaring the unit repaired. It had needed only minor adjustments.

Canby thanked the repairmen, then he buzzed Norris and asked for a ham sandwich and a cup of black coffee if anyone was going out for lunch.

No one was. Canby had a dried-out chicken salad sandwich and a cup of lukewarm coffee from the downstairs cafeteria vending machines.

While he was eating lunch, Jennings from the lab came in and told him that the tapes of the extortionist's phone voice had been analyzed and that the voice was a woman's electronically distorted to sound like a man's.

Jennings was a jittery man with ruddy hands that had never learned to knot a necktie properly. His striped tie askew, he stood in the center of Canby's office and explained. "You see, by varying decibels and pitch—"

Canby interrupted the technical explanation with an impatient wave of his hand. "Is there any way you can bring out the original voice?"

"We tried, Captain. The voice wouldn't be an accurate reproduction to the ear, but we did make some voiceprints. They're like fingerprints, impossible to disguise completely. Of course, I realize that for comparison you need a suspect."

Canby thanked Jennings and finished the arid chicken salad sandwich.

By one-thirty that afternoon, Canby had found out from the photographs what he needed to know.

When he looked down at the photograph Mathews had placed on his desk, his heart seemed to slow to stillness, and he realized why it hadn't taken long to obtain results.

"The job is all shit sometimes," Mathews said, standing to the left of the desk with his long arms crossed.

Canby told him to leave.

The air conditioner began to squeal loudly and Canby

struck it harder than was necessary to make it stop.

Minor adjustments, he thought disgustedly.

Sometimes major adjustments were necessary, regardless of the price.

36

1980

She loved again. That had taken her by surprise, had been unplanned. Now she was involved with a different sort of man, and with a different sort of love.

It was a love not at all like the love she still felt for her husband.

It was a love that could injure but couldn't maim.

She could endure the pain of leaving it.

37

The Present

Within ten minutes Vera Kivas was seated in Canby's office.

She calmly smoked a cigarette and stared at him with level, bold eyes. If she was afraid, she hid it well.

"Why?" Canby asked her simply.

"A million dollars."

"But you spent years on this."

"A million dollars," she repeated in exactly the same tone, as if the words were some sort of religious incantation.

Canby shook his head. "Even with the stakes that high, it had to be something more."

"Is there more than a million dollars?"

Canby knew what she meant. Wasn't the mythical "million" really, for a while anyway, the goal of almost everyone? Even though almost everyone realized that goal would never be reached. But Vera Kivas was experienced enough to have long ago set aside that symbolic goal. Unless she was one of those who could never set it aside.

"Originally it was Dimitri's idea." she said. "I tried to talk

192

him out of it but failed, so I went along with it. He showed me where he was going to plant the explosives, in the angles of steel I-beams where pipes went up, after the beams were wrapped with insulation. And in soon-to-be concreted areas of remodeling projects." For the first time a warm light of emotion entered her eyes. "We were small people, of common origin, but Dimitri didn't think small or common. And I learned from him. He made me believe."

The warm light dimmed, became a cold tinsel glitter, as she continued. "Then came the cancer. I never dreamed he could die . . . so suddenly. Death is more than anything a surprise. And there I was, more alone than I'd imagined possible. That kind of loneliness was as much a surprise as the cancer."

Canby sat for a suspended moment in the silence with her as she thought back to that time of her life. He knew that outside the door were several armed patrolmen, to make sure that Vera Kivas remained found.

"But Dimitri had completed the initial stage of the operation: the explosives were in place. He'd planned for everything but his death. I suppose I was carrying on what he started, in a sense keeping him alive. Keeping us both alive. Giving me purpose. For both of us, it was something I needed to finish."

"You even got a job with the Police Department, wangled your way into the precinct you knew would be involved in the investigation, made a fool of the man you anticipated would control that investigation."

"The last part I didn't plan." She drew on her cigarette as if the act brought about a pain that was somehow necessary. "The night your car exploded . . . the phone call was to be sure you *wouldn't* be in it. I don't expect you to believe me, and I don't blame you."

Still the fool, Canby thought, realizing that he believed her. "You came close, Molly," he said with more than a trace of admiration. "For a girl born into a world like yours, you came close."

"Better than close."

Canby glimpsed again, nearer the surface, the steel he'd occasionally perceived in Vera Kivas–Molly Garrity.

She actually smiled, not gloatingly, but as if she were about to best Canby in some trivial game.

"When Dimitri died," she said, "I knew I'd need help to carry on his plan. I have a confederate."

Canby wasn't surprised. What Molly had embarked on was simply too big for any one person. There was, he'd long ago discovered, a limit to what the solitary conscience could contain.

"My confederate is talking to the mayor at this minute," Molly went on in a soft, earnest voice. It was the same voice she had used to profess her love for Canby. "The mayor is receiving specific instructions about delivery of the money, and instructions about my immediate release. If both sets of instructions aren't strictly adhered to, another building will be destroyed along with its occupants."

Her expression hadn't changed when she told Canby this.

"Molly!"

"I mean it, Dex."

A terrible sadness washed through him, and he felt a sense of loss so acute it was like something sharp deep in his bowels. "What are the instructions pertaining to your release?"

She smiled, as if things had been set right again. "Simply that I be allowed to walk out of here unhindered in any way. Of course," she added, "you'll have me followed." They both knew that no one person in a city as large as New York could be followed indefinitely if he or she was aware of the fact.

"Do you really think I can let you walk away from here?"

"Do you seriously believe you can do anything else?"

"So many people, Molly, already dead. And now you're threatening more. Is a million dollars worth that? And if this is your way of keeping your husband alive in your mind, won't he be dead even to you when this is finished?"

Her face contorted for a moment as if in a spasm of agony,

and Canby knew how much strain she was actually under. Again he couldn't help admiring her, and he cursed himself for it.

"I want you absolved of responsiblity, Dex," she told him, ignoring his questions. "Phone the mayor."

Canby did as she instructed and was put through immediately to Mayor Danner.

"I was about to phone you," Danner said. He seemed out of breath. "Is what I was told true?"

"Vera Kivas is sitting in my office now."

The phone almost jumped in Canby's hand. "Dammit, Canby, isn't there any way we can hold her?"

"That in itself would be simple."

Danner sighed. The sound was like rushing water in the receiver. "Let her walk," he said. "But stay on her, so close that you can tell what she's thinking."

"It's impossible to follow her indefinitely," Canby said, glancing at Molly. "She knows that."

"What about planting some kind of homing device on her?"

"She knows about that sort of thing too."

Danner's voice flattened out with his frustration. "Then all we can do is what she says when she says."

"For now, yes, sir."

"All right, Captain. . . ."

"I'll phone you back," Canby said, and hung up.

He nodded to Molly.

She seemed to want to say something, but instead she nodded back at Canby and stood. He watched the play of light on her dyed red hair, the balanced movement of her hips as she walked out the door without speaking or looking back. It was as if his future were exiting before his eyes and he could do nothing about it.

Canby gave the order to have her followed. Then he sat with his fingertips pressed whitely against the flat desk top, trying to sort his staggered emotions. His heart raced with a

195

strange irregularity, as if each beat were followed by an echoing beat.

He realized that more than anything else he was jealous of a corpse.

After a period of lost and unmeasured time, he picked up the phone and called Mayor Danner.

Danner told Canby the scenario for the next morning as related by Molly's confederate.

The extortionists would choose a cab at random and send it to the mayor's sister's apartment building so that it would arrive before 11:30 A.M. Simultaneous with the cab's arrival, the phone would ring and whoever was to deliver the money would be given the destination to tell the cabdriver.

Mayor Danner and Canby agreed that as things stood their wisest course of action was to see to it that nothing could go wrong during the delivery.

The cab, of course, would be followed, in case it was stopped en route. And its destination immediately would be staked out with extreme caution by the department's top men. At this point it was impossible for Canby and Danner to formulate a detailed, aggressive strategy; they could only seize opportunity when and if it presented itself.

When the mayor had hung up, Canby phoned Mathews and told him he wanted all information obtainable learned in the shortest time possible concerning Vera Kivas, a.k.a. Molly Garrity. That information would be available now. He instructed Mathews to put every man he could spare on the assignment.

After his conversation with Mathews, Canby sat and stared at nothing while what had happened sank deeply into his consciousness, permeated every fiber of mind and body. When he glanced at his watch, he was surprised to see that almost an hour had passed.

Very slightly shaking his entire body, as if shedding water, he got up and went out into the squad room to surround himself with people. Human presence and activity helped him to mourn less painfully for Molly. Canby knew that he was mourning for her; he recognized the familiar wrench of that emotion.

Molly Garrity no longer existed.

She was as dead as his first wife, Bernice.

38

Harold Vish hadn't gone home to his wife last night. He had, in fact, been gone since the morning before, when he'd left to meet an editor who was trying to woo him into publishing a collection of his reviews. Vish and the editor had gone to an early lunch that consisted mainly of martinis, and after the meeting Vish had run into an old friend at the Biltmore Carriage House and continued drinking.

Evening had found him soused. Outside the Biltmore he had almost been run over by a determined succession of cars on Madison Avenue. But he somehow managed to hail a cab and returned to the Beymer Building.

The cab ride had sobered him somewhat. He stood outside the Beymer Building's entrance and glanced at his wristwatch. Eight o'clock. Early.

Vish went inside and walked with what he thought to be a surprising degree of steadiness into the coffee shop. He ordered an open-faced beef sandwich and a salad. Myra saw that he'd been drinking too much and added a cup of black coffee to the order. As he ate, she refilled the cup frequently.

Soon Vish's hunger was appeased, but he felt the throbbing beginnings of a painful headache. And the inside of his mouth was bitter from too much coffee.

What he needed, he decided, belching softly, was a drink. A small one, to help him descend to sobriety without a hangover. He said good-bye to Myra, left an uncharacteristically generous tip, then walked from the coffee shop and crossed the lobby.

One of the elevators was at lobby level. Vish stepped in and pressed the button for the twenty-ninth floor, where Helice Gorham's apartment was located. As the elevator rose smoothly, he rested his head against the cool metal wall.

When she answered his knock, Helice told Vish that she'd just decided to settle down for the evening with the best-selling novel she held open in her hand.

But it wasn't a book deserving of its reputation or sales figures. She changed her mind.

If Helice Gorham and Harold Vish got little sleep that night, James Boston got even less.

The next morning, while Helice was nibbling with enthusiasm on Vish's earlobe, Boston was asleep in his armchair near the air-conditioning vent. Arlo was curled near Boston's slipper-clad feet, gazing disconsolately with his muzzle flat against the carpet. It was almost ten o'clock. Usually by this time Arlo had received his morning snack.

On the other side of the wall, Helice lay back, draped her sheer nightgown across her midriff and closed her eyes lightly. Beside her in her bed, Vish said, "God, I'm paying the price for yesterday."

"I take it you don't feel well," Helice said.

"I hardly feel at all."

She reached over and patted the angle of his pelvic bone. "Why don't you go home?"

"I have no compelling reason to."

"Wilma."

"Wilma is hardly compelling."

"It's after ten o'clock."

"I am beyond time."

"But Wilma isn't. If you've been gone as long as you say you have, she's liable to phone the police."

Vish knew Helice was right, but at the moment he couldn't bring himself to care. He realized that he'd decided, sometime between yesterday's drinks, that he was going to leave Wilma.

"I'm going to leave her," he said.

"But you haven't yet." Helice sat up and pulled her gown on over her head. Her hair was unbelievably tangled yet somehow flattering. "I don't want you found here."

"Why would anyone look for me here?"

"Don't be naïve, Harold. It's difficult to keep a complete secret anywhere, much less in this building."

Vish watched her rise, then he managed to struggle to a sitting position on the edge of the mattress. "I suppose you're right," he said, waiting for his head to stop pulsing. His tongue was dry, and a dull reminder of hunger stirred in his stomach.

"I'll make some coffee and orange juice while you're getting dressed," Helice said. She put on a robe and walked from the bedroom.

Vish sat and listened to the sounds of preparation coming from the kitchen. Then, with great effort, he stood. Grasping a corner of the dresser for momentary support, he made his way into the bathroom and beneath a warm shower.

Gradually he altered the water temperature until the shower was cold, and by the time he stepped from the opaque-glass stall and toweled himself dry with a large pink towel, he felt considerably better. He dressed and walked into the kitchen, his mood raised by the aroma of freshly perked coffee.

Helice had two cups of coffee and two large glasses of orange juice arranged on the Formica top of the small breakfast bar. The glasses were fancy, gold-rimmed cylinders adorned with intricate etching.

As Vish lifted his glass to drink, he saw with amazement that the etching was pornographic.

"I see I rate the good china," he said.

"I've had those for years. My first husband gave them to me, along with a number of other interesting items. I'd throw those away if they weren't good crystal."

Vish nodded at the wisdom of keeping such glasses and finished his orange juice.

"Did you mean it when you said you were leaving Wilma?" Helice asked.

Vish took a sip of coffee and burned his tongue. "I meant it."

Helice moved to the other side of the breakfast bar so that she was directly facing Vish. "Harold, don't do something like that on my account. We can continue as we are indefinitely."

"It's Wilma I can't continue with indefinitely," Vish said. He smiled at Helice. "You're as much effect as cause."

She nodded and looked away from him. She had brushed her hair and was now her usual artfully groomed self. As she picked up her juice glass she asked, "When are you going to tell her?"

"As soon as I get an opportunity."

"Where will you go?"

"Temporarily, to a hotel." Leaving his coffee cup nearly full, Vish walked into the living room and found his suit coat on the floor near the sofa. It was so absurdly wrinkled he decided to carry it rather than wear it.

Helice had followed him from the kitchen. She stood behind him, leaning the length of her body against his, her right arm encircling him. He felt the warmth of her breath on his back as she spoke. "Think about it some more before you tell Wilma."

"That's no way for the 'other woman' to talk." Vish said. He turned and kissed her, surprised to taste the salt of her tears. He hadn't imagined crying to be in her repertoire.

"Helice," he said, still gripping her upper arms, "I have

201

given it a great deal of thought. But I always arrive at the same conclusion."

"I should have expected something like this," she said.

"Didn't you?"

She let a long breath escape and nodded, somewhat sadly. "I suppose I did. You can't dance without expecting that sooner or later the music will stop."

"It isn't stopping for us," Vish told her. "It's stopping for Wilma."

"I'm crying for Wilma," she told him as he went out.

Vish took an elevator up five floors, then walked along the carpeted hall toward his apartment. If Wilma was in the apartment he would tell her now that he was leaving. If she wasn't there, he would begin to pack. The quicker and cleaner the break, the easier it would be to heal.

He unlocked the apartment door, stepped inside and stood motionless. Then he walked slowly about, staring incredulously.

But for his study and the kitchen, the apartment was empty. Bare. Vacated. Vish felt a burgeoning, resigned sort of anger.

Wilma had left no note. But in the center of the kitchen table lay a single frozen fish.

Vish stared at the frost-coated fish in wonder.

He'd never dreamed Wilma could be so adept with symbolism.

39

When she was ready, Molly easily saw to it that she would no longer be followed. For most of that day she'd made herself simple to keep track of, so that when she was ready to lose the men assigned to trail her they would be somewhat lulled and caught off guard.

Just after five o'clock, when the streets were flooding with office employees and traffic was almost at its nightly predicament of horn-honking immobility, Molly entered Korvettes department store on Fifth Avenue.

It was easier to move through the store than along the more crowded sidewalks outside, and she was reasonably sure that the men following her would comply with procedure and cover all the building's exits. Running through the aisles to a side exit onto Forty-seventh Street, Molly was confident she would emerge unseen before her followers, who were pressing through the mass of pedestrians, could reach the point of the exit outside the building.

After breaking into the milling throng on the sidewalk, she

quickly and breathlessly walked half a block. Then she entered another building and cut through the lobby to the next street. A cab carrying a single passenger was sitting motionless in stopped traffic, its horn sounding an occasional futile note that was absorbed by the background of urban noise.

· Molly approached the cab, showed police identification and climbed in beside the startled passenger. He was an elderly man in a wrinkled brown suit. His lips began to shape words of protest, then instead formed a confused smile.

"I have to get to West Forty-fourth Street," Molly told the taxi driver, and instructed him to drive down a side street where traffic was moving. He showed her an unhappy face in the rearview mirror, shrugged and obeyed.

When the cab became bogged down again at a hopelessly tangled intersection, she paid the frustrated cabby, mentioning that the department would reimburse her, and instructed him to apply part of the tip to the other passenger's fare. Then she got out and began walking.

By the time rush-hour traffic had begun to thin, she was positive she was no longer being followed.

Unless telephone instructions were to the contrary, Canby would be the one to deliver the suitcase full of cash. Not only was it his responsibility, but he better than anyone might be able to deal effectively with Molly in a crisis situation.

He'd arrived at the mayor's sister's apartment early that morning, and the wait had begun.

The wait was now hours old.

Ordinarily the apartment would have been a pleasant place to wait. It was a large, ground-floor co-op unit, richly furnished, with a beige carpet and graceful cream-colored furniture. The ceiling-to-floor drapes also were beige, and transparent. Through them Canby could see the ornate ironwork that protected the windows. Though the apartment was set back only about twenty feet from the street, traffic noises were almost inaudible.

With Canby was Mayor Danner, his assistant, Carl Gaines, and two uniformed policemen from the seventeenth. The mayor's sister had wisely gone to visit a friend as suggested.

Outside the building, plainclothesmen waited patiently. The block was covered in all directions. When the cab sent by the extortionists drove away with Canby and the money, it would be followed. If some totally unexpected development occurred, the police would be ready.

Danner was seated in a dainty wood-trimmed chair that seemed about to splinter beneath his bulk. He'd taken off his suit coat and loosened his tie. Gaines appeared cool and only mildly concerned as he paced with his head bowed, as if searching for some small object he'd dropped on the carpet. Canby sat on the curved sofa, trying to relax as he thought about the positioning of the men outside and wondered if he'd overlooked something vital. Everyone needed for the waiting to be over. The imposed inactivity was unbearably straining already taut nerves.

"I can't feel comfortable with the idea of actually paying," Gaines said, pacing back from the window.

Danner sighed and rolled up his sleeves. "So you've told us, Carl."

"It's not only the political side—"

The telephone's shrill ring interrupted Gaines, stopped him in his pacing as if he'd encountered an unexpected barrier.

All three men were standing now. Canby slipped his earphones on and deliberately let the phone ring three more times before nodding for the mayor to answer.

The message was brief: A cab was on the way. It would arrive momentarily and honk, and the suitcase containing the money was to be taken to the cab by one person. That person would get into the cab and direct the cabby to drive to La Guardia airport. The passenger with the money must say he is on police business, then hand the cabby the suitcase and instruct him to open it. This to ensure that the suitcase won't be booby-trapped, and to impress upon the cabby the urgency

205

of reaching La Guardia without delay. Timing is important. At La Guardia, the person with the suitcase was to carry it to the bank of public phones near the American Airlines ticket counter and wait. One of the phones would ring and the caller would relay further instructions.

Almost casually, the voice on the other end of the line added, "Something will happen momentarily that will assure you that you have no choice but to follow instructions. What will occur can happen over and over within minutes, in every area of the city."

The line went dead and Canby removed his earphones. He knew what the caller had in mind, and an icy current of despair passed through him, for a moment constricting his throat and suspending his ability to speak.

Another building was coming down. Both as a convincer, as the caller had said, and, just as importantly, as a diversion, another catastrophe to stun the senses and render occupied and inefficient the machinery of the law.

Canby understood the caller's strategy. And horrible as it was, the strategy was sound. Make everyone wait, then keep them moving fast, unexpectedly, so it would be impossible for them to anticipate and plan.

Canby took the phone from Danner's hand, depressed the cradle button and dialed a number. He said one word: "La Guardia." And when he hung up the phone it began to ring.

He knew what he was going to hear this time on the other end of the line. Canby didn't want to pick up the receiver again, but he forced himself.

The voice on the phone was all the more chilling for its official, controlled recitation of the facts.

Explosions had been set off in a building on Fifty-seventh Street. The building's exact address wasn't yet known.

But this time something hadn't gone as planned. The building hadn't collapsed.

It had shifted on its foundation and might at any moment thunder down to a mass of body-filled rubble. But, so far, strained steel and concrete had held.

Canby gave orders to rush everything available to the scene of the explosion, but to leave the men assigned to the extortion money pickup in their present positions.

A horn was honking impatiently outside the building entrance.

Canby hung up. He swallowed the dry, persistent fear in his throat. He had to move fast. Now.

Danner and Gaines both wished him luck, but Canby barely heard them. He was moving toward the door, carrying the compact but heavy brown suitcase, trying not to think about how much money was at the end of his arm. The phone was ringing again behind him. He knew that this time it would be for the mayor, more information concerning the latest building detonation.

One of the uniformed officers held the door open for Canby and he walked down the narrow hall toward the foyer. He could see beyond the glass front doors to the street the yellow-orange bulk of the waiting Checker cab that Jericho had sent.

Canby looked only straight ahead as he strode to the cab and got in the rear seat. The cabby was a sleepy-eyed, swarthy man with a ragged mustache and a detached mood about him. He sat relaxed, with a wrist draped over the top of the steering wheel.

"Police," Canby said, showing his identification. "Drive to La Guardia and make time. Here's why." He followed instructions to the letter by handing up the suitcase.

The cabby appeared dumbfounded as he accepted the heavy suitcase and lowered it onto the front seat.

"Open it and look inside," Canby ordered.

Shrugging heavyweight shoulders, the cabby obeyed. Canby heard the soft teakettle shriek of his intake of breath, saw his neck crane forward and down.

"It ain't real," the cabby said, quickly closing the suitcase and snapping the latches as if there were something dangerous and alive inside.

"It's real," Canby said.

As he spoke, Canby's body jerked back against the soft seat, then flew forward.

A car had tapped the cab's rear bumper. The dreaded unexpected had occurred.

Canby looked out the cab's rear window and saw a dark-haired woman in a ridiculous wide-brimmed hat, behind the wheel of an Oldsmobile, raise her hands in helpless apology.

"Fuckin' woman drivers!" the cabby said in disgust, moving to open his door.

"Forget her," Canby said sharply. "It isn't serious anyway. Go!"

The cabby handed back the suitcase and put the cab into gear. Canby was pushed back again into the seat as they accelerated, whipping with easy precision across two lanes of traffic. A cluster of pedestrians about to cross an intersection halted in irregular, accordionlike sequence, bunching together just off the curb, giving ground to the speeding taxi.

Canby sat back, the suitcase resting on the floor between his feet, and tried not to think about what might be happening at the scene of the explosion-wracked building.

He thought instead of the upcoming exchange of money, the moment of ultimate risk in any extortion attempt. At that single, necessary and all-important point, for at least an instant the extortionist had to stand revealed and vulnerable. For the first time, the law would know when and where their quarry could be found. No matter how clever and delicate would be the exchange, money and extortionist had to converge. And if the law could be there simultaneously, the operation would be blown.

The problem was that the extortionist knew all this too. And was the one laying down the rules.

The cab shaved a corner and barely missed being sideswiped by a slow-moving delivery van, but Canby didn't notice.

40

At the time of the explosion, the coffee shop in the Beymer Building was beginning to fill with the early lunch-hour crowd. Ray and Gary had stopped in five minutes ago for the chicken salad special. They were seated near the end of the counter with only two glasses of water before them.

Mrs. Charmene, the elderly widow on the thirty-fifth floor, had phoned twice about the toast and tossed salad that was to be delivered to her. One more phone call to the coffee shop and Myra was sure that Mrs. Charmene would refuse to tip. Or maybe she would tip a nickel. She had done that once to Nel the part-time waitress, as a not very subtle complaint about the slowness of the service.

Nel was due in but hadn't arrived, so Myra fastened the styrofoam lid on Mrs. Charmene's order and asked Ernie the cook to watch the counter while she delivered the toast and salad. She would only be a few minutes, she said.

"Myra, sweet! Where you going?" Ray called after her, but

she ignored him as she hurried out from behind the counter and toward the exit to the lobby.

She stepped into the elevator and pressed the button for the thirty-fifth floor. The steel sliding doors hissed smoothly closed and the elevator began its ascent.

Then something strange happened. There was a rumbling from below, deep and sharp enough to hurt Myra's ears. The elevator seemed to gain speed as it rocketed up the shaft. Myra dropped the styrofoam-covered plate and fell back against a side wall, her stomach sinking and turning.

The whole thing seemed as if it took a long time, though actually only seconds were passing. Myra stared at the floor indicator above the closed doors. Every numeral was lighted and flickering.

Then suddenly she was weightless. As the elevator reached the apogee of its ascent, her body came away from the steel floor and wall. For an instant she scrambled in panic on her hands and knees.

The elevator began to plummet, to shudder and jar violently as it picked up speed. The overhead light blinked and went out, leaving Myra in total darkness. She tried to stand but lost her balance and fell back to the floor.

There were several severe jolts in quick succession, and the elevator slowed, then stopped with such suddenness that Myra's body was compressed against the floor, then hurled upward. Her right arm slammed against the closed doors, stung, then went numb. Pain burned along her entire left side.

There was another sound then, like large hailstones pattering on the elevator roof. The pattering became a hammering, then a roaring, and the elevator lurched downward another ten feet.

Sobbing, Myra awkwardly gained her feet and reached through darkness to caress the four smooth walls that confined her. *What had happened and why?* With the heel of her uninjured left hand, she began to beat on one of the walls, barely able to hear the blows being struck. Then, bracing a foot against the waist-high handrail, she desperately raised her body and felt for the service door on the elevator's roof.

The roof was buckled from some great weight atop the elevator; the service door was immovable.

Myra sat down on the floor and leaned her back against the closed sliding doors, suddenly aware that the air in the dark elevator was becoming stale. Each breath left a dull and yearning ache in her lungs. She knew, with a sad, surprising calm, that she would never leave the elevator alive.

Ernie was about to set the chicken salad specials on the counter before Ray and Gary when suddenly, for an instant, the laws of the universe were no longer in effect. Ray and Gary were airborne, their knees on a level with the counter-top. Behind them, on the other side of the coffee shop, a man seated eating his lunch was rising chair and all, still intent on his meal, his mouth gaping to take a bite of the half-eaten sandwich in his poised hand. Most astounding of all to Ernie during that fraction of time were the chicken salad specials, suspended motionless and unsupported before his eyes, like props in a magic act.

An ear-aching, dull hollow sound seemed to originate within Ernie and emanate in all directions, but he knew that was impossible. He could actually *see* shock waves, and see furniture, walls, people, react to their instantaneous passing.

Then the floor buckled, opened upward like a ruined draw-bridge to allow a terrible, pulsing thing beneath to encompass and obliterate everything, everyone.

As he sat toiling over his model sailing ship in his subbasement apartment, Metzger felt only a keen-edged surging pain and surprise, not fully realized.

On the Beymer Building's thirty-fourth floor, Harold Vish fell out of bed.

An earthquake, he thought immediately. He had once experienced similar shock waves on the West Coast.

The bed in his study was vibrating madly, its heavy oak legs actually bouncing off the floor so that Vish could see a thread of light between carpet and wood. That sliver of light, so incongruous, so unnatural, frightened him.

After returning from Helice Gorham's apartment early that morning, he had sipped half of a final drink and gone to sleep. Now he lay on the pulsating floor and watched the half-empty glass on the nightstand near the bed. The stale scotch diluted by melted ice was vibrating and splashing against the sides of the glass, like a tiny amber sea in turmoil.

From below came a distant roar, then a horrible shifting, rending noise. The dresser mirror cracked diagonally with a sound like a rifle shot and reflected a scissured, disjointed room. Vish stretched out his arms and dug his fingers into the carpet. His fright drove a low, wavering moan from him.

Then the motion, the vibration, stopped. Only the irregular pounding of Vish's heart filled the room.

He lay for a long time, clinging to the solidity of the floor, before struggling to his hands and knees. Then he drew a deep breath and stood.

Immediately he knew that some subtle yet fundamental change had occurred. He took·a tentative step, staggered slightly, then stood with his hands on his hips. A glance out the window at the peaks of the opposite buildings told him that everything beyond the windowpane was as before.

Or was it? There might be a slight, almost unnoticeable difference in the view, something that escaped ready explanation.

When he took a step toward the nightstand to toss down the rest of the scotch, he stopped and stared with a sudden cold fear. The liquid in the glass was unmoving, but like the liquid in a carpenter's tilted level, it was at a marked angle with the top and bottom horizontal planes of the glass. At an angle with the horizontal planes of the nightstand top, the floor. Not a great angle, but nevertheless an angle.

Vish backed away from the glass as if afraid of it, turned and hurriedly put on his shoes and his wrinkled shirt from the night before. He had slept in the rest of his clothes.

212

Within a minute he'd opened his apartment door and stepped into the canted hall. He had to get to Helice's!

Though the angle of the hall floor was slight,Vish held on to the wall with one hand as he made his way toward the elevators. Apartment doors were opening up and down the hall; frightened, puzzled faces peered out.

"Mr. Vish, what happened?" an apprehensive voice said behind him. Mrs. Mallory from 34B. Vish ignored her.

When he reached the elevators and pressed the down button, the indicator lights above the closed doors remained dim. It suddenly occurred to Vish that the only illumination in the hall was from the two tall windows at the corners. Of course the electricity would be off!

Behind him there was movement in the hall, the buzz of questioning, fearful voices. Vish walked quickly toward the fire stairs, noticing in the faint light that the hall walls were traversed by wide jagged cracks. A fine grayish powder from the separated wallboard coated the carpet and the glossy leather toes of his shoes like pale dust.

The door to the stairs was jammed, but he slammed the bottom of his foot against it and it opened.

The cement stairs were dim, cracked, littered with debris. Vish propped the door open for as much light as possible and started down.

As he descended he came across more debris, sections of cement from the stairs above, from walls and the ceilings of landings. Below him the stairs were more brightly lighted.

When he reached the bright landing he paused and had to hold on to the banister to overcome his nausea. A section of the building's outer wall had fallen away to reveal a breathtaking expanse of blue sky. Climbing gingerly over the rubble, careful not to look into the dizzying void, Vish continued down. He saw that he'd cut his hand, but he couldn't remember where or how. As he half stumbled down the next flight of uneven stairs, he wrapped an expensive handkerchief about the bleeding hand.

Then he squinted through the dimness. The door ahead

was clearly marked "29" in large yellow numerals. Vish gripped the metal handle and pulled on the heavy door, expecting it to resist. But it swung open easily and he stepped into the twenty-ninth-floor hallway.

He made his way through the milling, frightened twenty-ninth-floor occupants toward Helice's apartment door. The air was thick with a gritty, acrid dust that set the teeth on edge.

A hand clutched at Vish's shirt-sleeve. He was about to brush it away when he looked down and saw that it was Helice's hand. She was beside him, staring up at him. Her expression was calm, almost amused, but there were tear streaks on her makeup.

"We seem to be crooked," she said.

Vish held her against him and couldn't be sure if she was trembling or he was. "Do you know what happened?" he asked.

She shook her head. "No one knows exactly. But everything outside seems normal. It's only this building. An explosion . . ."

From directly above their heads came the muffled, shuffling beat of many feet moving swiftly. In panic? Helice gripped Vish's arm and squeezed until the sound abruptly ceased.

A slender, elderly man was standing against the wall next to Vish and Helice. He was holding a small schnauzer almost casually beneath one arm, as if about to take the dog for a walk. "Someone has gone to see if the stairs are clear," he said. He was staring at Vish and Helice with a curious glazed expression that suggested he might be in shock.

There was a stirring at the east end of the hall, desperate voices, then a tumult of movement wildly exaggerated by long shadows. A woman began a loud, rhythmic weeping.

It didn't take long for the message to sweep along the crowded hall. The stairs were blocked with tons of rubble two stories below, impassable. The elevators were inoperable, their shafts stopped with debris above the ruined elevators themselves.

"We're trapped," Helice said softly to Vish.

"No, there must be a way out."

"We're on the twenty-ninth floor, Harold!"

From below, very faintly, came the forlorn wail of sirens.

"We're all going to die," the man holding the dog said in a voice crisp with bitterness. "And only some of us deserve to."

41

Molly sat patiently, waiting for the money. She was listening to the news chattering from a small radio with a cracked plastic case. The Beymer Building hadn't fallen.

She knew that didn't matter. The effect of even its partial demolition was enough for the purpose of the plan.

Molly had no compelling reason to care if the Beymer Building fell or remained standing.Yet she knew that she did care. She wanted very much for the building to come down. That realization was unsettling to her. All these years, had it been mainly the money she was pursuing? Or something else that had only occasionally shown itself in hazy glimpses? Retribution? Justice? An irrational desire that others should join her husband in death?

She told herself that now she could face whatever was necessary, offering no excuses or apologies, succumbing to no guilt.

Molly sat and prayed for the Beymer Building to fall. She could do that without the slightest sense of incongruity.

* * *

Vish saw that many of the people crowding the twenty-ninth-floor hall of the Beymer Building had gone back to their apartments for various valued objects. A short woman in a tight pants suit was clutching a handful of glittering jewelry; a man behind her was holding a small, graceful piece of modern steel sculpture; anther woman was cradling a bulky fur wrap. Toward the other end of the hall, Vish even glimpsed a neatly dressed man carrying a large framed painting.

It all struck Vish as absurd, like a bad piece of business in a play destined for early closing. Didn't these people comprehend the gravity of their predicament?

The gravity. His unintentional pun for some reason reverberated through Vish's mind and threatened to bubble from his lips in a low, horrible chuckle. For a moment he thought that he actually *had* laughed, but when he looked about he saw no evidence of anyone having heard.

42

As the Checker cab wended through traffic on Park Avenue, Canby realized why the building on Fifty-seventh Street had been chosen for destruction. It was easily visible from the cab's window as the route to La Guardia was followed.

But where Canby was meant to see only an awesome gap where the building had been, there the building itself stood.

Canby recognized the towering modern structure. The Beymer Building.

And what he saw was even more frightening than the void he was meant to see. The building was leaning at nearly a 15-degree angle, and even as Canby stared from the cab window he could imagine that the mass of steel and concrete was slowly toppling, crumbling and roaring down along with the people still inside. Postcard pictures of the gravity-defying leaning tower of Pisa created that same dizzying expectation. He wondered how many people still were in the building. And how many had been killed outright in the explosion.

Then Canby saw the three tan National Guard helicopters

edging across blue sky toward the angled building, and he knew that the tenants on the upper floors must be trapped. Helicopters would be the only way to get them out, from the roof. And if they were trapped in large numbers, the task of removing them all would be monumental.

The cabdriver had noticed the helicopters and the startling angle of the building they were approaching.

"Jesus, what happened over there?" he said in an awed voice.

"Nothing to what's going to happen if we don't get to La Guardia soon," Canby told him.

The cabby stared straight ahead at the snarled traffic.

The traffic diverted from the area of the Beymer Building made the cab's progress slower than on a normal day. Canby sat nervously in the back seat, watching pedestrians a few feet away stream past unimpeded while he remained motionless. He had to conquer the impulse to leap from the cab and begin walking. Under usual circumstances he could have made better time that way, walking out of the congested area and hailing another taxi farther down the block. But he knew he had no choice but to stay where he was, to follow his instructions exactly. The cab continued to gain ground by inches rather than miles.

Finally the curb lane of traffic began moving steadily. At the first corner, the cabby wheeled onto a side street, detoured three blocks out of his way and drove south on Second Avenue, where traffic was moving at an almost normal pace.

When at last they arrived at La Guardia, Canby quickly paid the cabby and climbed out of the taxi, his grip firm on the suitcase handle. The cabby accepted the fare along with Canby's generous tip and stared at the suitcase as Canby walked swiftly toward the terminal building. When Canby was out of sight, the cab accelerated into the stream of traffic leaving the airport and headed back toward the city.

Canby glanced at his watch. The trip to La Guardia had taken twenty-six minutes. Not as long as it had seemed in the stuffy confines of the cab's rear seat. The American ticket counter and the bank of phones were just ahead. He made his way nimbly through the purposefully striding crowd of the terminal building, one of hundreds walking hurriedly carrying a nondescript suitcase. The public-address system was droning unintelligibly, and there was a crescendo of jet engine roar as a plane took off.

Most of the dozen phones near the ticket counter were being used. Canby sat down in one of a line of chairs near the phones, placing the brown suitcase beside him on the floor and letting his right hand rest on the handle.

Across from him a pretty, dark-haired girl in a stylish green dress was reading a paperback novel. Two seats to the left sat a harried-looking man in a blue suit, gazing absently and gnawing his lower lip. To Canby's right sat a blond man in plaid slacks and a red sport shirt, reading a newspaper with the casual interest of someone trying to pass time. No one seemed to be paying the slightest attention to Canby.

Canby glanced toward the ticket counter and saw Art Shammler, the detective lieutenant in charge of the airport operation, standing with a light raincoat over one arm and an attaché case and garment bag at his feet. Shammler was smoking a cigarette and seemed like nothing so much as a traveling businessman killing time between flights. Canby hadn't had time for a precise rundown on how the watch at the airport was set up; it was possible that one or more of the people seated near him or using the phones might be members of Shammler's detail. And it was possible that one of those near Canby would make a move to pick up the money.

Or perhaps Canby would receive instructions over the phone simply to leave the suitcase and walk from the terminal building, allowing the pickup to be made just before a departing flight that would transport the courier thousands of miles away. Canby hoped they might try to work it that way; it would make things comparatively easy.

He stopped speculating, resting his back against the chair and keeping alert for the ring of one of the phones. He found himself thinking of Molly, and of the Beymer Building.

The Beymer Building was a haven for the very wealthy, for whom Molly had often expressed an almost militant disgust. Canby knew that she regarded people born into and raised in wealth as insensitive and selfish. And the Morgell Trust Building had been, after all, a bank. Perhaps Canby shouldn't have been so surprised by Molly's revelations.

Canby wondered, Who was Vera Kivas, really, before she'd married Dimitri? Had she been born into relative poverty, as had Canby himself? If so, he could more easily understand what she'd done.

His mind balked. He did not formulate into words the thought he was reaching for: He could more easily forgive her.

Another departing flight trailed thunder overhead.

Canby glanced again at his watch.

Fifteen minutes had passed.

43

Time seemed to move in irregular sequences, relative to hope.

Instructions to turn on portable radios had been conveyed to the trapped Beymer Building tenants by police using powerful electric bullhorns. Radio station WNYC would provide them with information.

In the hall on the twenty-ninth floor, several battery-powered radios were produced almost immediately.

The tenants learned that everyone below the twenty-second floor had been evacuated. Workmen were toiling now to clear away some of the rubble in the stairwell to allow access from the upper floors, but it appeared that any breakthrough would be hours away. There was no danger of fire, and everyone was urged to remain calm.

Overhead were several National Guard helicopters with harnesses that would be lowered to roof level. Evacuation of the trapped tenants would be conducted by helicopter until other rescue operations began to show signs of progress.

"Or until the building collapses," someone said in a voice suggesting near-panic.

Without air conditioning, the interior of the Beymer Building had soon warmed to over 80 degrees. Sleeves, even pants legs, had been rolled up, and several men had stripped off their shirts.

"Only a few should go onto the roof at one time," the calm, patient radio voice was saying. "If everyone moves onto the upper floors, the difference in weight distribution might cause the building to shift even more on its foundation."

But already everyone was edging toward the stairs leading to the roof. Vish gripped Helice's elbow and moved with the human current toward the stairway door. A trickle of perspiration ran down the side of his neck and inside his collar.

"Wait, wait!" someone screamed. "We need to have some sort of system!"

From behind Vish came a burst of loud, uncontrolled laughter.

The stairs were jammed with people. Quickly the tempo of movement picked up. Vish saw an upward stream of pale, frightened faces, pumping legs and elbows. Amid the disjointed rhythm of shuffling feet lay several motionless, silent forms, oblivious now, like mannequins that had been placed there for effect by a low-budget film director. No one spoke; there were only the sounds of shoe leather on hard cement, heavy, pulsing breathing and occasional frantic whimpering. The mass of sudden hope, of desperation, surged upward.

Vish was among them, struggling to hold Helice upright as they climbed the stairs. Something clutched at his ankle, but with a frenzied strength he pulled free and gained another two steps. Somewhere near him a woman was sobbing and wheezing. An elbow dug into his ribs, jarring the breath from him. He retaliated viciously, jabbing out wildly with his own elbow.

A section of cement fell away from somewhere overhead. There were a few brief, startled screams, the hail-like scattering of cement chips and dust over those directly below. Vish felt something small and hard strike his shoulder, momentarily numbing it, and for a while he was blinded by a thick haze of powdered concrete. Helice held on to the front of his belt, helping him stay on his feet as he was mashed and buffeted by the crowd.

They moved into an area of bright sunlight, and from overhead came the reverberating beat of helicopter rotors.

"Stay calm," a nasal, mechanical voice was shouting from one of the helicopters. *"Please remain calm!"* But the loud, fluttering beat drew everyone on with its staccato promise of salvation.

Then they were on the roof. Vish stumbled and fell onto graveled blacktop, stinging the heel of his hand as he caught himself, then immediately regained his feet. He clutched Helice's wrist and they moved quickly away from the jam of people at the roof's stairwell entrance.

Vish looked about and felt a sharp thrust of fear. Here the cant of the roof was quite visible. The building was tilted far enough to make him feel that he had to lean in the opposite direction to compensate.

"Please remain calm!"

Vish saw a woman being raised toward a hovering helicopter, the heavy leather harness encircling her beneath her arms, her bare legs kicking wildly. The helicopter was already moving away to make room for another with a dangling harness. Wind gusted across the roof, plastering clothes to perspiration-soaked bodies and fluttering dresses and shirttails.

"Please remain calm!"

From the window of surrounding buildings, faces peered across critical voids at the Beymer Building's roof. Most of the faces were immobile, frozen in expressions of detached helplessness, like faces of the dead. But across Fifty-seventh Street Vish saw a man wearing a full beard laugh, actually laugh. Strangely, Vish felt no anger at the sight. He felt instead a deep and grievous embarrassment for the man.

Vish guided Helice toward the center of the roof, where they were more likely to be picked up. The small elderly man who had been staring at them downstairs in the hall crowded ahead of them. Incredibly, he was still carrying the miniature schnauzer. He ran a few steps to maintain distance between himself and Vish, not looking back.

Another helicopter was hovering lower, trailing its harness on a thin, umbilical cable. Everyone on the roof stood motionless, head tilted back, gazing upward.

The helicopter dropped still lower, growing surprisingly huge. There was a scramble where the harness touched down.

Several men shouted as the helicopter rose slowly on its thrashing blades. A heavy-set woman, clutching a child, dangled in the harness at the end of the cable that was being wound on its winch, drawing its human cargo toward the open helicopter door. Two green-uniformed men stood in the gaping door, leaning precariously forward and staring down at the woman and child as they drew nearer.

Another helicopter was circling in from the east, sunlight glinting through the shimmering arc of its whirring blades.

"Please remain calm!"

Vish glanced around him. There now were over a hundred people on the tilted roof. Easily over a hundred! And more were fighting their way up from the stairwell.

Helice gripped Vish's upper arm, leaned against him with her eyes closed as if she were dizzy.

"We'll be all right!" he shouted at her over the pulsing beat of the approaching helicopter.

She nodded, not looking at him.

He realized that he didn't actually love her, any more than he'd loved Wilma. He did feel a great pity for her, and for himself. And he was glad that Wilma had left him in time to be safe. He was slightly taken aback by that magnanimous impulse, but he knew that he really was glad for Wilma.

The helicopter was almost directly above them now, but the harness it trailed still was too high to reach. The slowly twisting harness was moving toward the center of the roof as it tantalized, drifting lower.

Vish and Helice unconsciously moved toward the lower-

225

ing cable, but they knew they had little chance of reaching it. Where the harness dipped the final ten feet to within reach of grasping hands, there was a burst of shouting and movement.

Vish felt a slight trembling beneath him as he stared upward at the marvelously buoyant helicopter. The helicopter seemed to rise smoothly and swiftly at an angle.

"Please remain calm!"

Vish knew! His heart was something wild that thrashed and swelled to such proportions that it blocked his breath. He became barely aware of screams and a growing remote thunder as his stomach rose and his weight lightened on the soles of his shoes. The windows of surrounding buildings soared upward in intermittent, wildly accelerating streaks. Then the wide surface of the Beymer Building roof tilted drastically if gently, and there was nothing beneath Vish's feet as everything whirled about him and he flailed his arms and legs to seek nonexistent solidity.

A numb acceptance supplanted panic. The speed of descent increased with merciful rapidity. Even above the crashing, madly increasing din, Vish was aware of the press and roar of the wind.

44

In his apartment, Strother had sat watching the televised account of the Beymer Building's predicament. In the brief space of sky between the two buildings on his TV screen, the oddly insectlike form of a helicopter appeared and disappeared. The camera withdrew for a longer shot of the leaning building.

Squinting at the screen, Strother had tried to perceive any change in the angle of the Beymer Building. He'd decided that anything but a major shift of the structure would be impossible to discern on TV. And that sort of shift would surely bring complete disaster.

But the building still stood, and the Morgell Trust Building, Strother's building, had fallen. It was insane of him to place any blame on himself, he knew. Yet almost a thousand people might disagree—if they were alive to do so.

Ann walked in from the kitchen, carrying two cups of tea.

"God," she said, "I feel like a ghoul looking at that TV. Watching, waiting, being sold cold tablets in between."

Strother took a cup from her and she sat next to him on the sofa. He understood how she felt, and in a sense she was right. The building had to fall soon. No structure could stand at that angle for any length of time.

Of course, stress distribution could be a strange and unpredictable factor. Strother could only hope that by some freak of explosion-rendered support, weight and counterweight, the Beymer Building would stand long enough for the upper-floor tenants to be removed.

On the TV screen, an upward-angled camera shot recorded a high, distant figure being lifted on the end of an invisible cable trailing from a helicopter. Slowly the dark, writhing figure was drawn toward the helicopter, but the craft passed out of sight above the rooftops of surrounding buildings before the camera could focus on the two high objects merging.

Beside Strother, Ann was sipping her hot tea and ostensibly looking at the TV screen. But Strother knew she was observing him, concerned about what his reaction might be to what they were watching.

Why *hadn't* the Beymer Building fallen? he wondered again. Certainly the hand responsible for the destruction of the Morgell Trust Building was responsible for this latest atrocity. Perhaps time had deteriorated some of the explosives, and they hadn't detonated. Or perhaps, unless brought down legally and professionally, with all the manpower and visible aid usually employed in that type of operation, such buildings if designed and constructed capably simply could absorb the damage.

Strother stood and walked across the room, spilling some of his tea on his hand and on the carpet. He ignored the pain of the burn, not even breaking stride.

"Where are you going?" Ann asked.

"To make some phone calls. The blast areas of that building already have been examined close up by people involved in the rescue operation."

Strother knew that Canby wouldn't be available, would be caught up in his own personal dilemma while overseeing the extortion money delivery. But there were others he could phone, using Canby's name to find out what he needed to know.

He spent the next twenty minutes on the telephone.

Then Strother returned to the living room where Ann was watching news accounts of the Beymer Building ordeal. The tea was cold now, but he carried the half-full cup gingerly as if it were still warm. The muscles of his face, Ann noted, were somehow more relaxed. The fearful whiteness about the corners of his lips was gone.

"I know why," he said with a note of relief, putting down the cup and saucer. "Why the Beymer Building's still standing while the Morgell Trust Building fell. Five years ago a sub-basement was added to the Beymer Building. It must have absorbed some of the force of the explosions, directed it downward."

But Ann seemed not to be listening. He noticed tears brimming her eyes, and her slender hands were trembling in her lap.

"The Beymer Building came down," she told him. "It happened while you were on the phone."

Without looking at the screen, Strother walked slowly to the television set and turned it off.

Then he sat down next to Ann on the sofa and tried to comfort her.

45

Fifteen minutes had passed since Canby had sat down, and none of the public phones near the American Airlines ticket counter had rung. He remained seated, idly stealing glances at the bank of phones to make sure that the unlikelihood of all the lines being tied up at once hadn't occurred. The blond man still sat to Canby's right, reading a newspaper with mild interest. The harried businessman type in the blue suit still sat nervously gnawing his lower lip. The pretty girl in the green dress who'd been sitting across from Canby had hurried off five minutes ago, lugging a many-pocketed tote bag on a long shoulder strap, and been replaced by a bearded man wearing a T-shirt lettered "Lonely? Me too."

Canby had removed his hand from the suitcase handle, but he sat with the calf of his right leg pressed firmly against hard vinyl. For some reason he felt better if he remained in physical contact with the suitcase.

He looked toward the ticket counter and saw that Shammler was still standing as if patiently waiting for the time of his flight to draw near. Shammler had never once glanced at Canby since Canby had arrived with the suitcase.

A graying, mustached man in an American Airlines captain's uniform walked through the crowded terminal lobby, carrying a red flight bag. He paused for a moment, smiled and said something to Shammler. Canby observed the brief conversation with seeming disinterest.

Shammler was visibly affected by what the man had told him. As the man walked on toward the departure gates, Shammler stood staring straight ahead with a faintly stricken expression, his face blanched.

Then he seemed to return to normal and calmly lit a cigarette, absently flipping a small silver lighter into the air and catching it before returning it to his pocket. He didn't look at Canby.

Canby glanced again at his watch. Twenty-five minutes had passed since he'd sat down. From the corner of his eye he saw Shammler stroll over to the ticket counter and talk for a moment with one of the reservations girls as if settling some question in his mind about his flight. The girl smiled at him as they talked, then turned and busied herself with some papers on a nearby desk. Canby knew she was an undercover policewoman. He looked away from Shammler and couldn't help diverting his gaze downward to his wristwatch once more.

Shammler's conversation with the woman behind the counter had taken less than a minute. The slowly passing segments of time marked off by the watch seemed to pile up piece by piece to exert increasing pressure on Canby. Shammler continued to check periodically with the girl behind the counter.

When forty-five minutes had passed since his arrival at La Guardia, Canby stood, wiped his forehead with the back of his hand, picked up the suitcase and paced briefly to relieve some of his nervousness and to stretch cramped muscles. Then he sat back down in the same chair and stayed alert for the ring of one of the nearby phones.

After an hour had passed, Shammler dropped his cigarette,

deliberately and with practiced grace ground it out beneath the toe of his shoe, and walked over to where Canby was sitting. Casually, as if killing time by looking for someone to talk to, he sat down in the chair beside Canby.

"Enough time?" he asked, and tapped a rolled-up *Newsweek* on his knee.

"Not yet," Canby said, surprised and annoyed by Shammler's indiscriminate actions.

"The Beymer Building is gone."

It took a moment for the calmly stated news to permeate Canby's mind. "Sweet Christ! . . ."

"And I thought you ought to know what else we found out a few minutes ago, Captain. We've been checking on Molly Garrity as instructed. Her real name, her maiden name before she married Kivas, was Molly Carrigan. Vera was a nickname. She grew up the hard way in the slums down by the wharves. And she has a brother Josh, Joshua C., three years older than she is."

Joshua! "A brother?"

"Joshua C., and he drives a cab."

A cab!

The tension of waiting exploded from Canby's mouth in an inarticulate half snarl, half curse. Quickly he flipped the latches on the suitcase at his feet, laid it flat on the floor and lifted the lid.

He was staring at stacks of neatly folded newspaper.

Canby understood immediately what had happened. It must have been Molly, wearing glasses, a dark wig and that ridiculous attention-diverting hat, who was driving the car that had bumped Canby's cab outside the mayor's sister's apartment building. Joshua's cab. Probably she didn't realize Canby would be delivering the money personally and that had been quite a shock. But it had all happened fast and the plan worked.

Bumping the cab had been a diversion, allowing Joshua to switch suitcases and hand back Canby the duplicate filled with newspaper. After dropping Canby at the airport terminal building, the cab, and the money, had been quickly swallowed up in the thronging traffic interspersed with countless yellow-orange cabs like Joshua's. With something like the Beymer Building tragedy to occupy them, it wasn't likely that the police would follow a cab that had done nothing more than transport Canby to the airport.

Now Molly, Joshua, the million dollars, all had disappeared.

"Shit!" Shammler said, staring at the newspaper-packed duplicate suitcase.

An airliner roared low overhead, with a sound like rumbling, mocking celestial laughter.

46

On the drive back from La Guardia, Canby sat dismally in the rear of the unmarked car and assessed the situation.

Worse than the loss of the money,. and potentially worse than the deaths resulting from the destruction of the Beymer Building, was the fact that there still might be buildings scattered throughout New York that contained explosives that by some fluke might be detonated. For that matter, what was to prevent Molly and Joshua from coming back for seconds? What they had managed to do once, they probably could do a second time with less difficulty and risk. There would be no doubt in anyone's mind that they were serious.

What was needed was for them to be apprehended. With their arrests they could be made to tell where other explosives might be located. The pair could be tried and convicted and the city would be safe.

But Molly knew how the police worked. Of course, she didn't know for sure that some of the bills she and Joshua had received bore recorded serial numbers. Though certainly she would suspect that possibility. But she could only suspect . . .

Both Canby and Mayor Danner would be under heavy fire for cooperating fully with the extortionists. Canby actually smiled thinly in anticipation. Perhaps that full cooperation would in the end be justified. He hoped so. He'd hoped for nothing so much in his life. It would help to assuage the guilt he felt for vaguely pitying and admiring Molly despite the horror of her crime.

The car slowed as it encountered heavier traffic. Outside sounded a cacophony of horns. Canby was on Park Avenue. He knew that off to his right would be the striking patch of sky in the towering landscape of the city, the void that had been occupied by the Beymer Building. But he refused to look in that direction.

47

Mayor Danner's demeanor was that of a gambler who had played a desperate hand and lost. Openly now, his political enemies were demanding his blood, confident that they would have it.

Canby had to admire Danner. The veteran politician didn't seem primarily concerned with the fact that he was now virtually a lame-duck mayor. It was the statistics on the Beymer Building collapse that as he heard them seemed to drag at his features, harden his gaze and age his face and body as he sat slumped forward at his bare desk. Canby wanted to reassure the mayor, but at this point there was nothing he could say. And he was a man who could use some reassurance himself.

Unlike the Morgell Trust disaster, this time there had been the opportunity to evacuate most of the building and cordon off the area. Still, the figures, when considered in human terms, made the blood cool and a slow sadness and rage engulf the heart: 126 dead, including twelve firemen and three policemen, 37 injured. The low number of injured was the result of an almost 100 percent fatality rate among those who had come down with the building.

Silent, turned in his chair and staring out the window, Danner nodded Canby's dismissal. With a sense of relief, Canby stood and walked across the thick carpet.

Outside, the air seemed purer and easier to breathe. Leaving the mayor's office was like leaving the aftermath of an execution, that curious atmosphere of death and irretrievable elapsed time.

When Canby returned to his office at the seventeenth, Thorpe phoned. If Mayor Danner had appeared aged in his office, Thorpe sounded even more aged on the phone. There was no anger in his voice, only defeat. But Canby couldn't be as sorry for his old friend as for Mayor Danner. Thorpe's manner left little doubt that his defeat was largely personal.

Later that afternoon Strother phoned and insisted that Canby have dinner at Durell's that evening with him and Ann. Canby could tell that Strother had decided that he, Strother, was enduring what had happened better than Canby was and wanted to console, to thank, to reassure with platitudes he hardly believed himself.

Anticipated as they were, the consequences of the Beymer Building's destruction were being adequately attended to, as if a macabre routine had been established. Canby really wasn't needed; he existed now in a pall of inactivity. He sidestepped supper but agreed to meet Strother and Ann for drinks.

In the convivial surroundings of Durell's amid conversation, laughter, the clinking of glasses and silverware, Canby did feel somewhat revived. His life hadn't ended, only become less bearable.

The Molly Carrigan case (as he'd come to think of it) was the sort that destroyed not only its victims but people and careers on its periphery. Canby knew he could be counted among the latter. Yet in a far dark corner of his mind, his policeman's intuition was spinning a fine thread.

The waiter arrived with their drinks. He set Ann's whiskey sour before her, then served Strother and Canby. Canby sipped his double bourbon and savored its gradual, radiating warmth.

"We'll have to learn to live with what's happened because we haven't any choice," Strother said. He was wearing a dark sport coat and tie that made him appear almost funereal.

What a naïve thing to say, Canby thought. There was always a choice. Usually several. But often they were choices most people didn't care even to consider.

Ann was dressed in a pale gray blouse crisscrossed by a silver chain that hung about her neck. She appeared to have been crying. Canby noted anew that she was a beautiful girl, and guessed that beneath her beauty existed something durable and vital. He envied Strother.

"Do you think Molly and her brother will ever turn up again?" Strother asked. He'd ignored his drink.

Canby nodded.

"But they got away," Ann said.

Canby smiled a reflective, knowing smile over the rim of his glass. "Did they? Some of the bills have recorded serial numbers. I'm sure the Carrigans suspect that, but only suspect. And they grew up poor, Molly and her brother."

"Making them all the craftier," Strother said.

"They'll be turned up by the machinery of the law," Canby told him, almost sadly. "It's plodding, sometimes even stupid and unfeeling, but it is relentless. It grinds fine, like the mills of the gods. And now it knows who and what to search for."

Strother and Anne sat staring at Canby. He could see them striving to believe, to gain mental footing.

"The thing that compels some people to commit a crime," he said with assurance, "also compels them to be caught."

He lifted his glass, the man with nothing more to lose, proposing a toast. His wife was dead, the art of his youth had

238

dissipated rather than grown, the woman he had almost loved was gone, his career might well be over, and in the recesses of his conscience drifted a thousand featureless faces of the dead.

He would survive.

"To the machinery," he said.

48

Miami, Florida

Molly Carrigan stood staring into the jeweler's window at the expensive ring, a cluster of perfect diamonds in a dainty white gold setting. The sun seemed to rest like a burning weight on her shoulders and she felt slightly faint from the heat. Her hair was brown again, cut short, and skillfully applied makeup had drastically altered her appearance.

It had rained earlier that afternoon. It seemed that every day it rained in midafternoon; then the sky cleared and the heat would be intensified by the dampness of everything it touched. It was hot that way now, and Molly could hear the nearby sea pulse with the rhythm of her own heart.

She had spent most of her time during the past two months in various motels, where it was cool and increasingly monotonous. Joshua was gone. She didn't know where he was. That was their plan. They'd agreed from the beginning that it would be best to separate and keep their destinations secret. That way they could each feel secure in the knowledge that if

240

something happened to the other, no damaging information could be extracted.

Molly continued to stare at the glinting ring. Beyond the window the jeweler's showroom was dim and no doubt cool. The shop was just off Collins Avenue, one of the most exclusive areas of Miami, and most of the hotels and shops were kept extra cool for their wealthy clientele. It was during one of her lonely, infrequent walks that Molly had seen the ring, had been drawn to it.

She had always wanted such a ring, just such a ring. An understated but definite declaration of her wealth, of her importance. She and Dimitri had dreamed of him someday giving her such a ring, years ago. That ring—that very ring— Molly was sure. And now, in a way, it could be his gift to her.

Of course, some of the money might be traceable. Before spending such a large amount, she should wait for the money to be "laundered" or until a cooling-off period had passed. That, too, had been part of the plan from the beginning.

But it was also possible that the city had cooperated fully, that none of the bills were marked or recorded. Very possible. After all, every step of the way there had been full cooperation.

Molly hesitated in the steaming heat, debating whether to walk back to her motel or to go inside and look more closely at the ring. Then she nodded to the uniformed guard at the door and walked into the plush comfort of the exclusive showroom.

It *was* cool inside, she was pleased to discover. As dim and cool as a tomb. From close up, without the intervening plate-glass show window, the ring was even more irresistibly beautiful. It glittered with a personal, an intimate aura, her past and her future.

Smiling, subservient, a clerk hurried to assist her.

Later that week, Molly sensed that something was wrong as she was strolling along the path leading to the board walkway of the Sun-N-Surf Motel. It was almost as if the ocean were whispering to her to be careful. She stopped, stood poised, and in a moment realized what had aroused her sudden suspicion.

If she hadn't been approaching the motel from the rear, along the sandy path through the maze of irregularly spaced palms, she would have reached the motel, perhaps even her cabin, without noticing that something was different. But she always took this route to the cabin, and not entirely as a conscious precaution. More and more she sought isolation. Wariness had become a habit.

And from her high vantage point she saw the car parked near the rear of the last cabin. It was a strange place to park a car. Then Molly saw that the section of weathered fence running out toward the beach would conceal it from anyone approaching the front of the motel. The car was a light blue Pontiac sedan, and jutting from its right rear fender was a small, stubby antenna of the type that served shortwave radios. Molly had been involved in law enforcement long enough to be able to spot an unmarked police car.

She took a step backward and scanned the area around her cabin. Several swimmers were lounging on the beach, and there was a man in wrinkled casual clothes and a fisherman's cap tinkering with a jeep two cabins from her own.

Then she saw one of the sunbathers, a tanned young man with a beard, adjust his tinted glasses and speak into what she had assumed was a portable radio on the beach towel beside him. She knew now that what she had thought was a radio was a walkie-talkie and that the motel was staked out.

The diamond ring! Some of the bills she had used to pay for it must have been traceable! The ring had deceived her.

The important thing, she knew, was not to run. Molly turned and walked with seeming nonchalance back along the path that led several hundred feet to a short wooden flight of stairs ending on the sidewalk. Once she reached the street, she probably would be safe. Fear threatened to erupt into physical action, into wild flight, at any second. Molly's muscles seemed to take on a will of their own that only tremendous concentration could overcome.

But no voice demanded that she halt. No figure loomed from the stark shadows to confront her. No hand suddenly clutched her arm. She had been walking with her fingertips in her purse, touching the small revolver that years ago Dimitri had given her. Now, as she reached the sidewalk and lost herself in the comforting numbers of sauntering tourists, she withdrew her hand, waited for her heart to slow.

Within a few blocks fear was supplanted by frustration, then by a disbelieving, weary sadness. She had a little less than five hundred dollars in her purse, and on her finger was the diamond ring.

The rest of her money was hidden inside a slit in the back of the sofa in her motel cabin. But not hidden so well that the police wouldn't find it.

More than an hour passed before Molly realized that she was walking aimlessly. She had nowhere to go.

49

Canby looked up from studying the daily reports and saw Mathews standing inside the office doorway. It wasn't like Mathews to sneak up that way without knocking, but when Canby saw the expression on the lieutenant's face he waited to see what he had to say.

"Vera Kivas again," was what Mathews said.

Canby felt a coolness drop through him. "Where?"

"A Forty-seventh Street diamond merchant phoned and said somebody was trying to sell him the diamond ring pictured on all those flyers we handed out. Then he described the seller. The hair was different, but everything else fit. The Kivas woman. By the time the cruiser got there she'd left, but they tailed her to the Marrington Hotel on West Forty-fifth. She's holed up there now in a room on the twentieth floor, and she's got sticks of dynamite strapped to her waist. She's threatening to blow up the place if we don't give her a car and a half-hour lead time."

Canby was on his feet. "Phone over there. Have whoever's in charge tell Molly I'm on my way to talk to her."

"Besides the dynamite, she's got a gun, Captain. A revolver. She already took a shot at—"

But Canby was already out the door.

As he drove toward the Marrington, siren singsonging and portable cherry light flashing, he tried to imagine Molly's state of mind. Her brother had been found a week ago after he'd gotten drunk and talked too much to people he knew too little about. The Atlanta police had traced him to a rooming house, then shot and killed him when he tried to run. And the week before that, almost all of Molly's share of the money had been recovered in a Miami motel cabin. She'd had little choice but to return here to her home city and try to sell the ring on Forty-seventh Street, the biggest concentrated diamond market in the country. The dynamite she must have gotten from wherever she and her husband had stored it years ago. It had to be old dynamite, not reliable, according to the experts. But there was no way to know its potency for sure.

The block of West Forty-fifth where the Marrington was located was cordoned off. The evacuation of the buildings surrounding the old hotel was still in progress. Uniformed patrolmen held back a crowd that was becoming larger and, in an odd way, angrier. They knew who was being held at bay inside the cordoned-off area. Of course, there were the usual nuts who wanted to see another building blown up, but most of the crowd stood silent and grim. What occasional shouts Canby heard were demands for blood and vengeance.

He identified himself and was let through the sparse line of patrolmen. The situation was still developing, still in a dangerous state of flux. Several civilians passed Canby, hurrying away from the Marrington with expressions ranging from fear to annoyance.

The lobby of the Marrington was empty but for half a dozen officers and a tall, bewildered-looking man who needed a shave and was apparently the manager. A captain named

Everest was in command. He recognized Canby and turned from a group talking with the manager and approached Canby across the dreary tiled floor. He was a small, wiry man with a head of bushy gray hair and a youthful sort of swagger in his walk.

"Thorpe called," he said, when he was a few feet from Canby. "This one is yours."

Canby wasn't surprised. He wondered about Thorpe's motives, though. Was this supposed to be Canby's chance to redeem himself? To redeem both of them?

"What have we got?" Canby asked Everest.

The wiry little man glanced around as if to assure himself that all the pieces on a game board were in place. "She's in an outside room on the twentieth floor," he said. "The dynamite is strapped to her waist and she's got her finger on the detonator button. She's also got a gun that she fired once at one of the first officers on the scene."

"What about the evacuation?"

"It's about half completed. We don't want to panic anyone so we're doing it building by building. I've got men deployed around the hotel and on the twentieth floor. She can't get out, we can't get in, she's a human bomb." For the first time Canby noticed a thinly drawn desperation in Everest.

"What are her demands?" Canby asked.

"A car and a half-hour start without police interference."

"She knows better," Canby said.

Everest wiped his chin with a forearm. "She isn't thinking real straight."

"You talked to her yourself?"

"By phone. But she doesn't answer anymore. I think she knows it's hopeless. I think she's liable to do what she threatens."

"We'll try the phone again," Canby said. He walked to the desk. The manager, whose name was Carllendar, handed him a black house phone from beneath the desk and told him to dial the room number, which was 2056. Canby dialed. He let

246

the phone ring ten times before hanging up. He didn't want to let it ring longer. He knew how a jangling phone could affect someone on the edge.

"All right," Canby said, handing back the phone, "I'm going up to talk to her."

Everest nodded. "Remember about the gun."

"Stick here by the phone," Canby said. "I'll call down to the desk if I do any good." He got a passkey from Carllendar, then he turned and walked toward the elevators.

Two of the hotel's four elevators were at lobby level. Canby stepped into one and punched the "20" button. As the elevator rose, he wondered what kind of damage Molly could do with her dynamite. The building, of course, couldn't be brought down, but if she had enough explosives she might cause a great deal of destruction, blow debris for blocks. Her threat was deadly enough.

When the elevator doors hissed open on the twentieth floor, a uniformed cop with a walkie-talkie hitched to his belt was waiting for Canby. He was carrying a twelve-gauge riot gun besides his holstered regulation revolver.

"I'm Flaherty, Captain Canby. It's this way."

Canby and the admirably calm Flaherty walked toward an angle in the corridor. The carpeting was fairly new and their footsteps made no noise. At the right-angle turn were two other uniformed officers armed with carbines. They stared at Canby and Flaherty but said nothing. There was a controlled sort of fear on their faces.

"Down there, sir," Flaherty said, pointing to the left around the corner. "The third door." He stuck his head around cautiously, then stepped out. "It's all right."

Canby nodded, rounded the corner and walked soundlessly toward the darkly stained door numbered 2056. When he reached it, he stood off slightly to one side.

He knocked.

When there was no answer, he said loudly, "It's Dex, Molly. Can I come in?"

"Stay away!"

The voice from inside was faint, without conviction. Not like the voice he remembered.

"I'm coming in to talk to you," Canby said.

She didn't answer. He drew a deep breath, reached out an arm and tried the passkey. The lock clicked and he pushed. She didn't have the bolt thrown. The door swung open.

"Alone, Dex!" she said suddenly. A line and tone that must have stuck in her mind from countless action movies.

"Never more so." On legs gone rubbery, Canby stepped into the doorway and entered.

She was standing facing him on the other side of the room. He was shocked at the change in her; he remembered being shocked at the changes in his wife's appearance each time he'd visited her in the hospital before her death. Molly's hair was brown now, raggedly cut. Her eyes seemed somehow faded yet with pinpoints of unnaturally bright light. She had lost weight. Tendons stood out on her neck and the line of her jaw was sharp and hard.

The dynamite was strapped about her waist beneath her untucked blouse. It made her appear grotesquely pregnant. In her left hand was a switch hooked onto some wires running between two buttons on her blouse. In her right hand was a small revolver aimed at Canby.

"This is a pressure release switch," she said, but she didn't look away from Canby. "If for any reason my thumb leaves it, the circuit will be completed to the detonators of twenty-five sticks of dynamite."

"Where do you figure all of this can take you, Molly? You're familiar enough with the game to know that what you want can't be."

"It can be." Her jaw muscles flexed, giving her features an unfamiliar squareness. "You can make it be."

"But I won't," Canby said. "And you know I won't." He studied her carefully. The woman he'd known must be somewhere within her. She couldn't have been a complete counterfeit all the time they'd been together.

248

"I'm coming over to where you are," he said. "I'm going to hold my finger on that button while you disconnect the wiring."

Fear transformed her face like something alive and writhing beneath her flesh. "Don't!" Her cry was plea and command.

Canby took his first step toward her. His second.

"Stop where you are, Dex!"

"You know this is the only sensible thing," he said in his professional reassuring voice.

A spiraling pain, then a numbness jolted his right leg and he was on the floor, realizing that she'd shot him. From where he lay he saw her at an insane angle as she whirled and disappeared into another room. He tried to call her name but his voice had left him. He heard a faint sound, felt a slight draft move across the carpet.

The floor heaved beneath Canby and there was an abrupt, ear-ringing roar. Plaster fell in chunks and wisps of trailing whitish dust. Glittering shards of glass danced through the air to shower like scattered diamonds on and around Canby. He covered his eyes with a forearm.

For a moment or a minute, time seemed to have been displaced, as if jarred off track by the explosion.

Then Canby was aware of someone in the room with him. He rolled onto his left side and saw blue uniform, silver badge, stolid cop's face, Canby of twenty-five years ago: Flaherty.

Canby and the young cop stared silently at each other, eyes locked in a mutual comprehension beyond words. Then Flaherty spoke.

"Jesus, Captain, she jumped and detonated the thing on the way down. She never reached the ground. Part of the front of the building's gone."

But Canby knew that the dynamite had caused a minimum of damage in the way it had been detonated. He sat up, noticed blood.

The deafening, heart-wrenching explosion still seemed to echo among the high, sharp angles of miles of towering buildings.

In Canby's mind, along with other tragic and persistent sounds of the past, it would continue to echo.

Then the room suddenly was filled with people, talking, moving about, reaching to get him out of the broken glass on the floor. Helping him up.